USA TODAY BESTSELLING AUTHOR
DALE MAYER

Killer in the Kiwis

Lovely Lethal Gardens 11

KILLER IN THE KIWIS: LOVELY LETHAL GARDENS,
BOOK 11
Dale Mayer
Valley Publishing

Copyright © 2020

ISBN-13: 978-1-773362-74-8
Print Edition

Books in This Series:

About This Book

A new cozy mystery series from *USA Today* best-selling author Dale Mayer. Follow gardener and amateur sleuth Doreen Montgomery—and her amusing and mostly lovable cat, dog, and parrot—as they catch murderers and solve crimes in lovely Kelowna, British Columbia.

Riches to rags. ... Chaos again. ... Winning is important, ... at least for some!

Doreen is overwhelmed with joy when she sees all the volunteers who show up to help get her deck addition built. Most of the men are cops, friends of Corporal Mack Moreau's, and are happy to help Mack's special friend and the lady who has helped solve so many crimes for them with a spot of home renovation.

But before the deck improvement can be finished, duty calls, and the cops are called away on a case. *Another* gray-haired lady has dropped dead. Yet another heart attack victim is added to the long line of previous ones. And, of course, neither of these recently deceased women had a heart condition that would explain their sudden demise.

With her animals at her side, Doreen is determined to figure out what the ladies had in common, plus why and how kiwis keep popping up in this case. As she digs into the ladies' lives, the things Doreen discover are shocking, ... but not as shocking as the answer is to this riddle ...

Prologue

Wednesday Late Afternoon ...

ARNOLD AND CHESTER prepared to leave, each one of them holding on to one of Heidi's arms.

"That was a good thing you did," Mack said quietly to Doreen.

Doreen gave him a quiet smile. "Someone needed to help Aretha. Now, of course, I don't have a case to work on ..." She looked at Mack hopefully.

He stiffened and glared at her. "None of mine."

"Don't you have another case in progress?" Arnold asked her.

"No," Doreen said with a big smile. "I figured I'd look into these old ladies dropping dead."

"You are the gardener," Chester said, with that fat smile of his. "If anybody can figure out what kiwis have to do with that damn case, I'd like to know."

Doreen stared at him. "Kiwis?"

Mack sent a warning look to Chester, but it was already too late. Chester was too far ahead.

"Yep," he said. "A kiwi in the mouth."

"But only one of the women's mouths?"

He leaned forward and said in that thick heavy whisper, "Yes, but all three had one on their person."

Doreen grinned. "*Killer in the Kiwis.* I love it." That was so her next case.

Mack shot her a hard look. "You stay out of it," he said. "Cold cases are one thing, but my cases are another."

She grinned up at him impudently. "No problem," she said. "You've got, let's see, what? Twenty-four hours?"

Mack jammed his hands on his hips, as Arnold started to chuckle. Whistling, he and Chester loaded Heidi into the back seat of their RCMP patrol car, leaving Doreen with Mack.

Doreen turned and looked up at him. "So?"

"So, what?" he growled.

"Twenty-four hours? Forty-eight? How much lead time do you need?" she asked hopefully. He took a hard step toward her, but she no longer felt threatened by Mack. She looked up at him and grinned. "Come on. Forty-eight hours it is then. It's a deal. I'm on the *Killer in the Kiwis* case."

Laughing, she raced into the kitchen. She heard the front door slam as Mack walked out, and she knew he had to leave. He now had even more work to do at the police station. And that was fine.

She'd give him the two days but not a minute more.

Chapter 1

Forty-One Hours and Counting …

F RIDAY MORNINGS WERE usually spent at Millicent's garden, and Doreen needed something to do anyway, as she awaited the end of Mack's head start on the kiwis case.

Calling the animals to her, she put some coffee in a thermos and walked over to Millicent's garden.

Millicent sat outside, and, as soon as she saw Doreen, Mack's mother bounced to her feet with what seemed like endless amounts of energy for someone Doreen's age, let alone someone of Millicent's age. "Oh, it's so good to see you," she said. "Mack told me about what happened with the jewels I found."

Doreen rolled her eyes. "I'm happy to let that case go," she said. "That was a little rough."

"Hey," the older woman said, beaming, "I really appreciate what you did though."

Doreen smiled and nodded. "I didn't expect it to come out the way it did. I still need to have a talk with Nan about Aretha."

"Well, we haven't heard all the details yet," she said. "So, if you want to fill me in …" She gave Doreen an enticing smile, hoping that she could coax Doreen into sharing more info. Doreen was happy to oblige. As she weeded in the garden and cleaned up the beds, she told Millicent all about the case.

"That's so hard to believe," the older woman said in amazement. "And why would the jewels end up under my juniper?"

"Now that," Doreen said, sitting back on her heels, "I really don't know, except that Reginald hid them around the city."

"And is this the last of them?"

"Well, it's the one he came back to get," Doreen said. "And they were gone."

"Of course they were," Millicent said. "The tree he was looking for was gone."

"And, therefore, he probably didn't know if he had the correct location or if the tree had been downed and then the jewels could have gone into a compost bin or were tossed into the dump or something else. But he couldn't find them. He did look for his landmark, apparently around your place, as far as I understand though. And he did give it a good search, but it was rough going."

Millicent nodded. "We had pulled the tree out after the storm had split the trunk, and the jewels sat there for a while before we discovered them. So anybody could have come and found them first, and we wouldn't have ever known," she marveled. "Just think of all this going on around us, and yet we had no idea."

"Anyway, it's all good," Doreen said. "Heidi will pay for her crimes—however the court ends up deciding the matter—and Aretha hopefully will continue to live in and to look after Heidi's house."

"And that'll be good for Aretha too," Millicent said with a knowing nod. "That poor woman needs something good to happen in her life."

By the time she had done all the weeding, Doreen had run out of things to talk about. But Millicent was full of questions, and she kept peppering Doreen with a million of them. Millicent totally agreed with selling the jewels and turning it into a charity scenario. It had been one of the things that Doreen was a little worried about, as nobody could really lay claim to the jewels. The businesses involved had gone bankrupt, and then so many years had gone by that it was hard to determine exactly who should get any money. She still needed to talk to Mack about it, and that was a bit of a problem because he was avoiding her.

"And you have a buyer for the emerald?" Millicent asked.

That launched Doreen into Zachary Winters's story.

"Oh, that's so sweet," Millicent said. "We definitely need to make sure that Mrs. Winters gets that emerald."

"I know," Doreen said, "but we'll sell a few of the other gems too."

Millicent sighed. "If there aren't very many, maybe we could split those up. You get one. Mack gets one, and Aretha gets one."

Doreen looked at her in surprise. "Well, you know what? That's not a bad idea. Sell the big ones, then put those funds into the charity, and everybody else can have one of the smaller gems," she said with a shrug. "I have to get them appraised, just to see what kind of money we're looking for. Only that didn't work out so well the first time."

"It will now." Millicent clapped her hands in joy. "Who knew that by asking you to look into this, you'd solve it, and so fast," she said with an admiring glance at Doreen.

"I don't know," Doreen said. "Seems like it took forever to me."

Millicent smiled and shook her head. "And, by the way, I was given a whole bag of zucchini," she said. "Do you want one or two?"

"If I knew how to make zucchini bread," Doreen said, "I'd love some. I could use one maybe."

"I made zucchini bread too," Millicent said. "Hang on a moment." She hopped up and raced inside.

While she was gone, Doreen picked up the wheelbarrow full of all the weeds and walked it over to Millicent's compost bin and quickly emptied the wheelbarrow. It wasn't her compost pick up this week, so Doreen moved the wheelbarrow back against the shed and tilted it up, so the rain wouldn't collect in it. When she returned to the deck, the animals were all sitting and paying attention. She looked down at them and said, "Millicent said zucchini, not treats."

Millicent's laughter seeped out through the door. She headed to the animals and gave all three of them a piece of cheese.

"Wow," Doreen said. "I didn't know you were feeding these guys too."

"Not all the time," Millicent said. "But it's such a joy to have them around."

"They're such moochers," Doreen said with a laugh.

"It's all good," she said. "And, for that matter, this is for you." She handed over a couple baby zucchinis and a pack of something wrapped up in tinfoil.

"What's in the tinfoil?" Doreen asked, looking at it.

"Oh my," she said. "The best zucchini bread ever. Ask Mack. He'll tell you."

"This is your own recipe," she said, her mouth already watering.

"Absolutely," Millicent said. "I don't even plant zucchinis in the garden anymore because so much comes from a single plant. But I have friends who still plant it, and they give me enough every summer. I've already put seven loaves of zucchini bread in the freezer, so please take this one."

"What about Mack though?" Doreen asked. "I don't want him getting shorted of his share."

Millicent's laughter carried across the backyard. "He'd probably thank you for taking some," she said. "Every time I bake a batch, I give him a whole loaf. He's protesting that he can't eat it all, so I'm sure he's happy that you take some."

Doreen wondered about that because none had come her way. So, either Mack was eating it all or he'd frozen a bunch himself. But he never seemed to be sad about taking any from her. She smiled at Millicent and said, "Thank you. I'll enjoy it thoroughly when I go home."

"Good," she said with a smile.

And, with that, Doreen led her motley crew around the cul-de-sac and onward to home. With her animals in tow, following along behind her. It would be a busy weekend if she and Mack could get started on the deck like she really wanted to, but she was afraid that they still needed more supplies. On that note, she sent Mack a text. **Do we have enough to start on the deck?**

The response came back as, **Yes.**

When?

Probably tomorrow. I'll stop by later tonight.

She grinned at that. **Dinner?**

Have you got anything?

Maybe, she replied with a frown as she headed to her

house. **Let me get inside and check.** She disarmed the security and walked into the front room. Without the furniture and with everything still so clean, it was an amazingly spacious-looking house. She headed back into the kitchen, where she set down her goodies and put on the teakettle. Then she checked out the fridge. She still had a few leftover noodles that he had cooked for her, but she was short on meat.

Leftover pasta, plain, she sent out. **No meat.**

Mushrooms?

Yes. Why?

A happy face was his response.

She chuckled. **Does that mean dinner?** she asked hopefully.

Maybe. Be there around five-ish, unless you put more work on my plate. She could almost hear the growl in his words.

She smiled and typed, **No, I'm good. I just finished at your mom's.**

Right. You can fill me in on how that's going when I get there.

Immediately she got worried. Was it costing him too much? Because she really didn't want to lose that money. But, at one point in time, all jobs came to an end. Millicent's place didn't need that much work anymore. Doreen could probably keep Mack's mom's yard looking good by just going every other week for the same money, which would save them some money but would cost her. Frowning, she pulled out the sandwich fixings and made herself a huge ham and cheese sandwich, with her usual lettuce and tomatoes. On a whim, she sliced zucchini and put the raw zucchini slices on it too.

She stared at it and wondered, "Maybe that's a little bit too far."

Then she cut a piece of zucchini into little pieces and put it in front of Thaddeus. He walked over and eyed it from all angles before he reached down and pecked a little piece of it. Doreen ate her sandwich with the zucchini slices on it, then shrugged. "It's not that bad," she said to Mugs.

He sat there at attention, looking up at her. Seeing a little bit of ham and cheese sticking out of her sandwich, she broke off a little piece of both and gave it to him.

Immediately Goliath glided forward, took up a seat in the chair beside her, and stared at her intently. She groaned. "You guys, you have your own food."

And she knew that they did because she had fed them herself, but she gave Goliath a little bit of cheese anyway.

As soon as her sandwich was gone, she got up and made a pot of tea and then brought out the jewels. She should have done this first. She laid them all out and took some photographs, wondering just how this would work. Millicent had a good suggestion about the six little diamonds. Give Mack two. Maybe Doreen could keep two as well, and Aretha could have the other two. She might just sell them for outright cash, given her financial situation.

Doreen didn't know what she would do with the loose gems. Mack probably didn't want his allotment, but she had yet to corner him on this issue. Doreen felt like her two should go to Aretha as well. After all, Doreen's situation had greatly improved since she had first arrived in Kelowna. When Nan's antiques sold at Christie's, Doreen would have plenty. It was still hard to imagine that. Still, she needed to get these jewels appraised by somebody she could entrust with them. Then sell the emerald to Zachary. *But didn't he already pay for this once, some forty years ago?*

Almost as if he knew what she had been thinking about, the phone rang. It was Zachary.

"I hear you had quite the fun," he said in a jovial voice.

"Yes," she said. "Mystery solved."

"And I can't believe it," he said. "I heard bits and pieces of it."

"Well, until the court determines the case," Doreen said, "nobody can confirm anything."

"And does that leave the emerald available for sale?"

"Potentially it does," she said drily. "I still haven't gotten anything appraised."

"Of course not," he said. "And you don't want to use my appraiser, do you?" His voice held a note of humor, as if understanding full well why she wouldn't trust them ever again.

"No," she said. "Secrecy and privacy are everything in this business, and they have lost my vote."

"Good enough," he said. "It was a deviance from their usual handlings of such matters, what with the extenuating circumstances, but I understand how you feel. Could I possibly have a copy of the appraisal?"

"Why would I do that?" she asked suspiciously.

"Because I still want to buy the emerald for my wife," he said.

"Wasn't it already paid for way back when?"

"Yes, but my insurance covered the loss back then too," he said. "Too bad the emerald isn't the same value today that it was back then."

"True enough," she said, not understanding how any of that worked. "Amazing that you got your insurance to pay out, yet Aretha and her husband didn't."

"But I was big on insurance," he said. "And I had already paid for the gem, and I had a valid receipt, so that loss was covered."

"Fine," she said, "but, like I said, I still have to get the jewels appraised, and then I have to figure out what a good selling price is."

"What will you do with the money?"

"That's still up for discussion right now," she said. "Potentially a charity because a lot of fingers are in this pot, but nobody seems to have a legal claim to these other jewels."

"Understood," he said. "Any chance we could wrap this up soon though?"

"If I could find a trustworthy jeweler who can do the appraisal, maybe," she said.

"The diamond exchange," he said. "They're coming through town in a couple weeks. You might get someone there to do an appraisal right on the spot."

She asked, "What is that?"

And he explained about a trade show that came into the city once a year. As soon as she got off the phone, she looked it up. And, sure enough, they were coming to Kelowna in two weeks. She sent them a message, wondering if anybody could do an honest appraisal on some diamonds and an emerald as well as a single ruby. She hoped for an answer that day, but, chances were, it wouldn't be that fast. It never seemed to be that fast.

Just then, a knock came at the front door. She hopped up and walked to the living room, then opened the door, Mugs barking like a crazy man. Grabbing his collar, she tried to pull him back as she opened the screen door.

A tall, lean man with short-cropped hair stood there with his hands on his hips, his back to her as he studied her front garden.

"Yes. Can I help you?"

"I came here to deliver some wood for you. Mack sent me." He turned to look at her, and he had a hard look to his features.

She smiled and said, "Is that for my deck?"

He shrugged. "Well, they're decking boards that I'm not using," he said. "And I picked up a couple from other friends. A bunch of us did our decks around the same time and helped each other. And we still had some wood that we couldn't use, so I brought it here." He pointed to the back of his truck, and she exclaimed in delight.

"That's marvelous." She moved down the steps, letting Mugs sniff the new arrival.

The stranger reached down and let him smell his hand, then gave him a good scratch. Mugs, instead of being the watchdog he was supposed to be, rolled over onto his back and showed the new arrival his belly. The man laughed. "Not much of a watchdog, is he?"

Doreen smiled. "You'd be surprised," she said. "He might not look like much, but he's got hidden depths."

The man nodded absently and said, "Whereabouts do you want the wood then?"

She smiled and said, "Around the corner here."

And he looked where she pointed, then nodded. "I'll start unloading it."

As she watched, he made several trips and had brought over at least twenty boards. "Wow," she said. "I might have enough to get that deck done."

"When will you do it?"

"Hopefully I'll get started this weekend," she said. "I don't know how much we can get done in two days though."

"A lot," he said. "Me and my buddies did all our decks in a weekend. Show me where you are planning to put the deck."

She walked him around to the back, where he could see the spot that she had cleared out.

"If you're not going too high, and if you don't have big steps and supports to do," he said, "that's an easy job."

"Seriously?"

"Absolutely," he said. "I'll talk to Mack about it." And he lifted his hand in a wave and took off.

She wasn't exactly sure what that meant, and, of course, she'd forgotten to ask his name. *Why would he need to talk to Mack about it?* Still, she wouldn't worry too much because Mack seemed to be one with a big network of friends that she didn't have. She appreciated the fact that people were pitching in the stuff that they couldn't use anymore.

As she walked back into the house, she sent Mack a text. **More boards were just delivered.**

Chapter 2

Forty-Eight Hours Plus Five Minutes Later ...

DOREEN HAD BEEN excitedly counting down the time. Mack's forty-eight hours had ended at 4:20 p.m. by her calculation. She snickered as she looked at her phone. "I should call Mack now," she muttered. She'd sent him a text five minutes earlier, letting him know she was still here, that his deadline was up—and mostly to poke fun at him. But she figured that he'd left her alone on purpose for her to rest and relax—and to avoid answering her texts. She wasn't so sure that it did any good yet, but she had at least spent a fair bit of time chilling.

And pretty soon, she had hopes of getting some work done on the deck. But they still had to prepare the yard, right? As in, they had barely started by clearing out the sod. She had rested all Thursday, and today was Friday, and she was looking forward to getting something done on the deck construction tonight, maybe, and this weekend for sure. She probably shouldn't hassle Mack now, as he had been such a big part in her getting a new deck. Plus he planned to cook dinner for her tonight.

She opened her laptop and searched for anything on

Mack's current weird case with the kiwis. Mack wouldn't appreciate her poking her nose in. It wasn't a cold case, and that would make more trouble for her. But she still had the Bob Small stuff. She looked over at that basket and smiled. She also had all of Soloman's files. So she had lots to work on. Surely something in there could be of interest. Yet her mind kept going to the little old ladies who were dying. ... She remembered Mack saying that nothing appeared suspicious, but they were waiting on the autopsy on the last one.

How did one make a decision about who got an autopsy and who didn't? She sat here, her fingers thrumming on the kitchen table, as she went through the news of the day online by a local channel, but nothing related to the kiwi murders was listed. She was getting frustrated. A day of rest was one thing, but two days of rest was one day too many. Still, she had worked on Millicent's garden. That had helped to shift her mood and to otherwise occupy her.

Even though Doreen's house was clean, it could do with a sweep, and the bathrooms needed to be wiped down. She quickly finished both of those chores, and, by that time, she felt justified in sitting back and sorting through all the newspaper articles on Bob Small. She had so many articles that it was almost too much. She put them in chronological order and opened her laptop, then started a file with the dates and a list of victims. When done, she had what appeared to be forty-odd newspaper clippings, and yet a lot of them were reporting on the same victims. She found eight victims over a period of three years, and she frowned at that.

"That's like almost one every quarter," she muttered. She didn't understand the mind-set of a serial killer. Drug addicts needed a fix daily, but how could you be okay for three months or so and then find a need to go kill somebody again? It just didn't make any sense to her.

When her phone rang, it surprised her, making her jump. She looked at it to see Mack calling. "Hey, Mack. What's up?"

"I'm at the grocery store," he said. "We can have pasta, but what would you like with it?"

"I have no clue," she said in surprise. "How late is it?"

"Dinnertime," he said.

And she looked down at her laptop and gasped. "Oh my," she said. "I had no idea."

"I guess the question really is, do you care?"

"About dinner? No, I don't. If you'll do something with pasta, you know I'll love it."

"Good enough."

She hung up, then quickly packed up everything that she had out because Mack would be here in minutes. He was really good at getting his nose into things she didn't want him to know about. But, if he wouldn't share anything about the little old ladies, then Doreen wouldn't share anything either. As soon as she finished packing up, she heard Mugs whining and jumping at the door.

She figured Mack was already here. She frowned at that and wondered how he always made it so fast. She walked to the door, opened it up, and let Mugs out. But saw no sign of Mack. Frowning, she walked down to the front yard and looked around, but nothing was there. She turned back to Mugs; he was heading to the far side, where all the decking supplies were. Worried that somebody had come and was helping themselves, she raced over to see him sniffing along the boards.

"What's up, buddy?" She didn't understand his sudden

interest in the materials. But it could be as simple as a squirrel or a stray cat had walked on them. Just then, Richard stepped out of his front door and looked at her. Immediately a glare formed. She smiled sunnily and said, "Afternoon."

"It's almost evening," he growled.

"It's not that dark yet," she said, with an airy wave of her hand.

"What kind of trouble are you up to now?" he asked.

She snorted. "I was hoping for no trouble."

"No media," he said suspiciously, glancing around.

She smiled. "I'm not sure they know about the latest case," she said.

"Case?"

She nodded. *"Jewels in the Juniper,"* she said with a smile. And she guessed that the media had likely collected around Heidi's house, where Aretha lived, but not here at Doreen's house. She laughed. "They'll be back. I'm sure."

"Well, if you'd stop sticking your nose where it doesn't belong," he said, "we wouldn't have the media here." With that, he stormed inside his house and slammed the door shut.

She groaned. "I didn't do it on purpose," she called out. But, of course, he wouldn't listen to her. She followed Mugs, who was still sniffing along but heading toward the back of the house. She walked around and then did a complete loop around her yard, but nobody was here. "Mugs, come on," she said. "Let's go in."

He dropped his butt on the ground and looked at her.

"Mack's coming," she said. She knew his ears wouldn't lift, but it almost looked like he was paying more attention. In the background, she did hear a vehicle. She smiled and said, "Let's go see if that's Mack." And she sped to the corner on a run, knowing that Mugs would keep up behind her.

As she got to the front yard, Goliath had snuck out with them, and he sat on the driveway. She groaned at him. "I don't like it when you are out here on your own and never in the front where there is traffic," she said.

He stared at her with those big marble eyes, his tail swishing behind him. She reached down and scooped him up into her arms. And then Mack drove into the cul-de-sac and came up the driveway. Mugs was so excited that it was all Doreen could do with Goliath in her arms to keep Mugs off the driveway too, so Mack could drive in. Mack shut off the engine, then hopped out and bent down to scratch Mugs. "Glad to see you like it when I come by, little guy."

"*Little* guy," she retorted. "He's getting fat."

"No," Mack said. "He isn't. He's just perfect."

She groaned. "So says you. He may be perfect, but, at the same time," she said, "he's not getting any smaller."

"Maybe not," he said, "but he's doing just fine. And so is this guy." And he walked over to Goliath in her arms and gave him a scratch. Goliath immediately reached out and tried to grab his hand as he withdrew it. He chuckled, slipped a hand under the cat, and took him from her arms. "Now this guy," he said, "he's an armful."

He cuddled the cat for a long moment, and it was pretty hard to get mad at anybody who would pay that kind of attention to her animals.

She smiled and said, "Obviously work wasn't too bad if you got off early."

"Didn't get off early," he said. "I went in early, and that made all the difference."

"And always you have lots more work to do, I know,"

she said. "What did you bring for dinner?" She could see the bags inside the front seat of his vehicle. He dropped Goliath gently onto the ground, then walked back to the truck and grabbed a couple bags of groceries. "This is getting to be a habit."

"I know," she said. "I was thinking of that. I wonder if I should be paying you money for the food that you keep bringing."

He chuckled and said, "Since I eat at the same time, it's not an issue."

"Yes, but I get the benefit of the leftovers."

He brought everything into the kitchen, while she shooed the animals back inside. It was one thing to leave them outside with the kitchen door open, and it was another to worry about them wandering around the front yard and too near the street. As she walked in, she said, "Should I show you the wood that we got delivered?"

"I'll take a look in a bit," he said. He pulled out something that she didn't recognize.

She picked up the package, looked at it, and said, "What are these?"

He glanced at her and smiled. "A different kind of feta," he said. "It's not in a brine."

"Well, I didn't know that feta came in a brine before," she said, "so that doesn't really matter. But I've never seen it in this shape either."

"It's just dry," he said.

She looked at him. "So, are we having that for dinner?"

"More of a Greek pasta," he said with a shrug. "I picked up a roasted chicken, which I'll chop up. And we have black olives, fresh tomatoes, feta, and I'll do a little bit of an olive oil sauce."

"Sounds lovely," she said. "Hot?"

He nodded.

"So, slightly different from the pasta salads I used to get with the artichokes?"

"Absolutely," he said.

"Now that I remembered that dish," she said, rubbing her stomach, "I could certainly go for some of that too."

"Too bad," he said instantly. And before long, he had a pan full of pasta warming up and took big cans of black olives from his bag, draining off the liquid from two of them, cutting the olives into quarters and tossing them into the pan. And then he diced up several big tomatoes that were really fleshy.

She looked at him and frowned. "Those are olive shaped."

"Romas," he said. "They're a little fleshy or less juicy, and they go great for when you don't want the tomatoes to fall apart." He chopped them up, added them to the pan, then some mushrooms and a bit of olive oil, and sautéed it all together. She wasn't even sure what else he put in.

"Wait," she exclaimed. "What did you just add?"

"Diced garlic," he said patiently. Then he added big dollops of butter to it all and gently sautéed everything together, while he chopped up all the chicken breasts from the chicken. With that added in too, the aroma made her superhungry.

"Can I do anything?" she asked as she watched.

"A salad would be good, if you have anything to go into it. I forgot to ask."

She immediately went to her fridge and nodded. "I can do that." She made up a simple green salad with cucumbers and was finished at the same time he served up two large plates of pasta. With the two bowls of salad and two pasta plates, they sat outside on her tiny deck, and she smiled. "It'll be nice to have a big deck here."

"I'll take a look at what supplies we've got after this," he said. "Sounds like a lot has arrived since I saw the pile."

"In the meantime, you can tell me about the little old ladies too," she said.

He remained silent and gave her a secretive smile.

She groaned. "Don't go after the Bob Small stuff," she said, "because that's a big project."

His eyebrows shot up, and he glared at her.

She shrugged. "It's a cold case."

"It's probably thirty cold cases," he muttered. "If not three times that."

Chapter 3

Friday Dinnertime ...

"WELL, WITH LONG-HAUL truckers," Doreen said, "it's pretty hard to keep track of their routes and who they could have come in contact with. Easy to stay under the radar for decades."

"Exactly the problem," Mack said. "On top of that, a lot of issues helped killers who operate across the provinces. The lack of cooperation and information sharing among the authorities was a real problem. These cases are from way before we ended up with any of the tracking systems we have now. And before the internet too, so it's not like searching for information on these cases was easy."

"In other words, with a little bit of luck, he kept trucking across the country, doing whatever he wanted, without getting caught," she said, shaking her head. "So many families have been affected."

"So many families," he admitted.

"And the little old ladies?"

"No mystery there. One died of what we're assuming is a natural cause, but we're still waiting for the autopsy to come back on the last one."

"So the first woman had a heart attack and dropped?"

"It happens," he stated.

"It does as long as nothing was done to help push that heart attack forward."

"Like what?"

She shrugged. "If she was in bed, and maybe an intruder came, and she was afraid for her life or something..." Doreen said, grasping for straws. "I don't really know, but..."

"She was walking on the sidewalk," he said.

"And nobody came up behind her and yelled into her ear with a great big megaphone or something like that?"

His eyebrows shot up. "Well, I don't know that for sure," he said cautiously. "Nobody saw her fall. She was found dead on the sidewalk."

"Interesting," she muttered. "How many is that now?"

"Three," he said in exasperation. "But remember. Old people die."

She snorted at that. "Apparently, in this town, young people do too." He coughed out a laugh, but a grim look was on his face. "What about the other two?"

"No way to know yet," he said.

"Same circumstances on the street? But not expecting anything odd on the autopsies?"

"One in a parking lot," he said, "and one in a park. Looks like heart attacks."

"All alone, all unattended, and nobody saw anything. Right?"

He slowly lowered his fork, then looked at her and said, "That's what I was afraid of."

"What do you mean?" she asked.

"I was afraid that you would see it the way I saw it."

"As in, it's a problem, right?"

He nodded slowly.

"What are the chances of three gray-haired ladies— Within what? Five days?—all dying in a similar way and sharing what seems to be the same cause of death?"

"It happens," he said. "We just don't have the population where I would expect it to happen so closely together."

She pointed her fork at him. "You know what? That's a really good point. If we were in Vancouver with a population of maybe three million, or say Paris or someplace where we're talking eleven million people, the numbers of gray-haired ladies dying from a heart attack would be much higher. And then maybe you would get three who died without people around them in a public location in just a matter of days. But, in Kelowna, where we only have a population of 140,000 or so people within the city limits …"

He nodded. He reached out and stabbed his fork into the salad. "Nice salad."

"Maybe," she said, "but this pasta is much better."

"Maybe," he said, "but—"

"Don't change the subject," she said. "Is anybody calling foul play?"

He shook his head as he took another bite of a salad.

"Too bad," she said with a heavy sigh.

He gave her a sideways glance, and she shrugged.

"I have lots to work on," she announced. She could almost see the relief swipe across his face, and she chuckled. "I'm really not that hard to get along with."

"I'm not saying you are," he said comfortably, as he dug back into his pasta.

They ate in comfortable silence, and then she said, "If we're working on the deck this weekend …"

He nodded but didn't look up, busy working on his plate.

She leaned forward and dropped her chin onto her hands, then asked, "Will I be enough to help you, or do we need to get some men in? I don't want you working on the deck and hurting yourself."

Surprise lit his eyes. "So are you worried about me?" He looked at her and grinned. "You might find it a very expensive weekend if you are planning on bringing in laborers."

"I know," she said with a wince. "I was afraid I would have to hire people anyway."

"Don't worry about that," he said. "I've asked a couple guys, if they've got time, to come and give us a hand."

"Oh, wonderful," she cried out. "If anybody'll come," she said, her voice lowered. "Don't forget that I'm hardly the most popular person in town."

He chuckled. "You're more popular than you think," he said. "But what you don't realize is, if people come and do work and volunteer like that, we have to supply food and beer."

She stared at him in shock. "Oh my."

He nodded sagely. "And that'll cost."

She reached up a shaky hand and asked, "How much?"

He shrugged. "I don't know." He motioned at the bowl of bills and coins sitting atop her kitchen table. "You may want to sort that out and donate it to the cause."

She looked at the bowl and smiled. "I've barely thought about that yet. I did show it to Nan though." She stood on the deck to get it from the kitchen, when he reached across, grabbing her hand. "Eat first," he said.

She groaned. "Will it take much money?"

"Well, we'll pick up some beer," he said. "At least a couple cases. So that'll be forty to fifty dollars."

She swallowed bravely and nodded. "Okay. Go on?"

"We'll need food," he said gently. "And you can't make any, and I'll be out working. So generally we're talking about bringing in sandwiches or pizza."

"Okay," she said. "And how much will we likely need?"

"At least another thirty bucks in pizza," he said. "It'd be hard to feed very many people without at least a half-dozen pizzas here."

She swallowed again and said, "Okay." But she could see the hundred dollar bill sticking out of the bowl. She headed inside and snagged it, then put it down on the deck table. "I found this in one of Nan's coats."

He looked at it, stared at her, looked at the hundred-dollar bill, then at her again, and said, "Wow. I wish your Nan had left me some coats."

She chuckled. "Right. My biggest nightmare is that I've left something in the clothing before I sent it off to Wendy's."

"I doubt it," he said. "If you did, and Wendy found any, she would tell you. But, I know you, and you probably searched inside the lining."

"Well, I did on some stuff," she said, "because Nan was safety-pinning money on the inside of a lot of her garments."

He studied her for a long moment. "Why would she do that?"

"So she didn't have to carry a purse," she explained. "But, as for the coats, I don't know." She shrugged. "But I did find a bunch of money."

"Well," he said, "you'll need at least this hundred-dollar bill. I can see a fifty from here. You need to pull that out and be prepared to spend it too."

She drew in a heavy sigh and stepped inside once more to snag the bowl this time, then added the fifty to the hundred. "Do you think that'll be enough?" she asked.

He frowned as he studied it, yet he continued to eat. "I'm hoping so," he said. "But honestly, I don't know. You could have four guys show up, or we could have ten guys, and ten guys will eat a lot of food."

"Right," she said.

And he said, "Don't leave that bowl where they can get into it because, although they're all good people, that doesn't mean somebody won't be tempted when they see money lying around."

"I won't do that," she said. "I need to sort through this bowl again, as it is."

"I thought you would have already done that by now."

"Nan and I counted it one day real fast. However, I've been holding off on touching it again," she said. "It's almost like having a chocolate bar waiting for you, and you really want it, but, once you eat it, then it's gone. In this case, once I start spending what's in the bowl, then that money's gone too. It's like my emergency fund." She finished the last couple bites of her pasta. "That was excellent," she said. "And I'm full now."

"I'm not," he said. He hopped up and served the last little bit to himself. "But I'll finish this with no problem."

"Then I won't have any leftovers," she grumbled good-naturedly.

"No," he said, "you won't. I'll be here early in the morning because I don't know how long it'll take to get the groundwork done."

She smiled and said, "Good enough. I'll make sure I've eaten by the time you get here, so I can jump right in and help you."

"Do that and plan on pizza for the rest of the day."

"What about the beer?" she asked. "I don't know anything about it."

"I'll pick up some after I leave here tonight," he said.

She looked at the money, frowned, and then said, "You think the fifty will cover it?"

"Not sure," he said. He looked over at a twenty still sitting on top of the bowl and said, "Why don't you sort that?"

"I did pick up coin wrappers." She hopped up and went to the shelves by the printer and pulled them out.

Immediately she shuffled over a little bit, then pulled the bowl closer toward her and laid all the bills together, including the $150 she'd already set aside. Then she went through the coins, pulling out all the little stuff that wasn't cash money. And, because it was older money, she was surprised when she didn't see any loonies and toonies in there—Canada's one-dollar coins and the two-dollar coins.

Mack picked up the earrings and whistled. "Aren't they pretty," he said.

"I showed them to Nan, thinking she might want them back, but she doesn't."

He smiled, nodded, and said, "The rest of it looks like notes and business cards." He picked up the dainty handkerchief and raised an eyebrow.

She shrugged. "Nan did have a lot of admirers," she said. "That's all she would say. She told me it was from an admirer."

He chuckled. "She's had an interesting life."

"That she has," Doreen said. When she was done sorting the money, Mack helped her roll up the coins. "I have it written down somewhere how much I counted last time."

She got up and went to her notes by her laptop.

"It's $924 dollars," she read off, nodding. "Same count as I got tonight." She looked at the bowl and realized that her entire bowl of money could be gone soon with this deck project. That money bowl had been her security blanket for these last few months. She walked over and took two baggies from the cupboard, then put all the paper money together in one, taking out the $170 for Mack and sticking it under her empty plate. She put the jewelry in another baggie. Then she dropped both baggies into her purse. And then she added the rolled-up coins to her bowl and took it all to set atop her printer. "I'll go through the cards and notes later," she said. "And figure out what to do with the odd opal too."

"Good enough," he said. "With any luck, we won't need too much more than this money for right now. The decking boards delivery you got today is huge, so we'll do what we can this weekend, and then, when we run out of time, we run out of time. When we run out of supplies, we make a run to the store." He shrugged. "That is just all there is to it."

"Right," she said.

And, on that note, he got up, grabbed her notepad, and headed to the side of the house. She came with her list of supplies to date and followed. It took him an hour to mark off everything. He frowned as he stared at her list and then down at his notes and said, "We have some decking screws and bolts for the anchors, but we'll need some other screws." He wrote on his list as he spoke; then he nodded. "Okay, I'll take that $100 for supplies and go get that stuff and get the beer with the $50. And take the $20 for good measure."

"Sounds good," she said. She walked back to the table on the deck, where she had anchored the bills under her empty plate, and brought them, as requested, to hand over to Mack.

"You okay to let me have this?" he asked, looking at her.

She smiled and nodded. "I trust you."

He rolled his eyes and said, "Good thing." Then he pulled out $40 from his pocket. "I wanted to check in with you if you're still okay to look after Mom's garden? Or is it getting to be too much?"

"I'm fine," she exclaimed. "I was afraid you wanted to stop our arrangement."

"Nope, she's so happy to have it done and she loves your visits. She spends hours outside enjoying her garden, always has." He handed her the money. "That's for this week's gardening."

She stared at it in delight and said, "Maybe we will make it through the weekend after all."

"Well, we still need more supplies," he warned. "We only got a half of a can of deck sealant here. That'll do a skinny coat, but that's all."

"If you say so," she said.

"But we can see how far it goes first and then can get that afterward," he muttered.

And, just like that, he hopped up into his vehicle, gave her a wave, and left. He managed to leave without cleaning up the kitchen again. Chuckling, she walked back to the deck table and grabbed their dirty dishes. She could hardly ask him to clean up when he cooked too, especially considering that he had brought the groceries. Some things she didn't need to get too cranky about. She appreciated the fact that he wanted to shop and to cook for her. She knew something was brewing between them, but she wasn't too sure how big of a something.

Then she sent him a text. **What about your brother?**

Next weekend, he answered back. **He's coming to your place next weekend.**

She stared at it in shock. It was one thing to have this happen in the near future, but it was another thing to have a date. She gulped. Not a whole lot she could do about it. It was well past the time to argue about it now, as she'd pushed it off as long as she could. But the deadlines were running. She responded with okay and left it at that. She had taken a couple steps here, though she didn't feel very comfortable about them yet. But somehow they felt a whole lot easier with Mack at her side. He'd proven himself to be somebody very honorable. Hopefully he'd stay that way.

Chapter 4

Friday Early Evening ...

A S SOON AS Mack left, she headed back to her laptop, took one look at the kitchen, and groaned. "I guess I better do that first."

She quickly cleaned up the kitchen, putting away the rest of the food that he'd used, realizing how generous he was because he didn't buy just enough for a meal but he bought enough to leave her a little bit as well. She didn't want him to think of her as a charity case, but she really did appreciate everything he did. At the same time, it was a little frustrating that she couldn't do the same thing for him.

As soon as she had washed the dishes, she sat down with a cup of tea and brought up her laptop. What she wanted to know was what would cause heart attacks in little old ladies. And what relevance did the kiwis have? It's odd how all three were eating kiwis at their time of death. Unless it was murder, and each had one stuffed into their mouth by the killer, like one of them had, per Chester.

What she found led her down a rabbit hole. All kinds of drugs could cause heart attacks, as she knew from the death of Ed Burns. Of course, in that case, the drugs built on those with preexisting heart conditions. What she needed to know now was whether all three of these ladies had heart conditions as well, but how would she find that out? Mack hadn't given her any names, and neither had the news. She sent Nan a text, asking if she knew anything about the little ladies who had recently died. She came back with a response of yes immediately. Doreen picked up the phone and phoned her. "What do you know?"

"What do *you* know?" Nan said immediately, and then she gasped. "Is this another case?" she asked, absolutely thrilled.

"Probably not," Doreen said. "They all died from heart attacks, or at least that's what they're assuming until the coroner's report comes back."

"Well, Kimmy definitely had a heart condition," Nan said, "so that would make sense."

"Kimmy who?"

"Kimmy Schwartz," she said.

"Did she live there at Rosemoor with you?"

"None of them did," Nan said. "But there's a great fun group of us, all us oldies, so I know about them."

"What about the other two?"

"Well, Delilah … What's Delilah's last name?" Nan's voice drifted off as she thought about it. "Norstrom. Delilah Norstrom. I don't know if she had a heart condition or not," she said, "but Bella might have. Bella Beauty," she said with a sneer. "She was overweight and unhealthy, so I'm not at all surprised that she dropped dead like she did."

"Maybe," Doreen said. "I guess I'm a little surprised that three of them would have happened so fast. And they were all eating kiwis."

"Well, when it's your time to go, it's your time to go,"

Nan said dismissively. "And a whole group of them eat kiwis all the time. It's part of their 'groupie' thing they had going on. You could see them with kiwis almost every day."

"Okay, that's weird. The time-to-go thing? Well, I get that," Doreen said. "I really do."

"Have you got anything else that you're working on right now?"

"No," Doreen said. "I did catalog the newspaper articles on the Bob Small stuff."

"Right," Nan said, her voice picking up. "That's a big one, isn't it?"

"It sure is," Doreen said. Privately she didn't think she could do anything on that case which the police hadn't already done. And, with so many victims across the country—at one time Mack had told her that he knew of thirty-two murders attributed to Bob Small—so it would be almost impossible to connect them. But obviously this friend of Nan's had done what she could. "And that reminds me," she said. "If it wasn't for that friend of yours who pulled all these together …"

"That was Hinja," she said. "Hinja Rampony."

"And is she living here in Kelowna?"

"She's down in the Lower Mainland, I think. Haven't spoken to her in quite a while. She's part of the Rampony family though."

"And that is?"

"One of the old Kelowna families," Nan said. "You know how they feel about being the first here."

"But you were good friends, weren't you?"

"Yes. She used to stay with me when she'd come to visit the rest of her family."

"When did you last see her?"

35

"Oh my," she said. "Probably a dozen years ago now."

"Huh. I wondered if she's gotten any more information on these articles," Doreen said.

"Well, I'm probably due to give her a call," she said. "Why don't I ask her when I do, but no clue when I'll connect. It may take a few calls to actually reach her."

"Sure," Doreen said. "For all I know, this guy's been caught and spending time behind bars for the last ten years."

"I doubt it," Nan said. "But maybe he dropped dead from a heart attack." On that note, she hung up.

Closing her laptop, Doreen got up and picked up her cup of tea, then walked down to the creek. The water was definitely a bit higher today. And it was now nighttime, so it would get a little bit higher right up until about three in the morning, when the last of the melt was happening from the snowpack as it came down and hit this part of the creek.

With the animals beside her, she sat on the grass and enjoyed the settling evening light. "It's been a good day, guys."

Mugs walked over and half crawled into her lap. Goliath was happy to just sit beside her, and Thaddeus walked up and down the water's edge, clucking, like something bothered him.

"It's okay, Thaddeus," she said. "I know the water's higher than you were expecting. It's higher than I expected too."

She still had a pathway, but her little creek had grown and had started to eat up to the edge of the dirt and the gravel walkway. "I can't imagine," she said, "how much bigger this creek can swell because some serious water is here now." And, indeed, it flowed with such a force that she didn't want herself or her animals to get any closer.

"Thaddeus," she said. "Come back over here where it's safer." He looked at her and made that weird little laughing sound. She shook her head. "Thaddeus," and she dropped her tone into a scolding voice, "come back here."

He looked at her again. "*Hah, hah, hah, hah.*"

She groaned. "Please don't drown," she said. "I really don't want to lose you right now."

His wings flapped in the air, and he made another weird sound, but this time he obliged and came closer.

She smiled when he got to her legs and said, "There you go now. You should be safe." But, of course, she couldn't stop thinking about what he might have seen in the water. Hopefully it was nothing, and just the height of the water bothered him. But she got up and walked to the edge to check.

As she got too close, Mugs barked at her. She looked down at him and nodded. "Right. But you didn't bark at Thaddeus, did you?" she said. "It probably wasn't a good idea for him to get as close as he was."

From where she stood, she tried to peer into the water but wasn't seeing anything. She smiled and said, "I think we're good, guys. He didn't find anything." At least she hoped he didn't. She kept checking it out, but the water flowed so fast that she couldn't see into it at all. She moved back to the spot where she'd been sitting, when Mugs barked again. This time, he faced the pathway.

She frowned and looked to see several figures walking up and down at the far side. "They might have every reason to be there," she scolded him. "It's not our creek, even though we like to think it is." But still, she was curious. With the animals in tow, she walked up along the houses on her side of the creek until she stopped in front of the two young men, standing there on the opposite bank. They were obviously agitated.

"What's the matter?" Doreen asked them.

One guy shrugged and said, "I wasn't expecting the water to be this high. I was looking to cross the creek."

"Can't right here," she said. "A little footbridge is down a ways, but some of the wood's rotten. So if you fall in ..."

He shrugged, nodded, and said, "How do we get to the street?"

"Well, where did you come from? Because if you lived in one of these houses," she said, "you could have just walked around to the front of the house."

He looked at her in surprise, then back at the houses behind him, and said, "Well, we are staying there with some friends, but we were told to head over to the cul-de-sac on the other side."

As that would have been close to Penny's house, she nodded and said, "You have to walk all the way around then, so that won't be the fastest thing to do."

"And how do I get there?" he asked.

She shrugged and said, "You need to find one of the little bridges closer to you."

He asked, "You live here?"

"Yes, I do," she said. "Down a ways."

"Can we go through your yard to get to the front road?"

"Only if you explain to me why you aren't using the street in front of the house where you're staying," she said. "Because that would make the most sense."

"We don't really want them to see us," he said. "We were staying there, but some funny stuff is going on, and we don't want to get involved."

By *funny stuff,* she figured he meant drugs. She sighed

and said, "Come on then."

She didn't know how old they were. To her, they looked like about twelve though, which meant they were probably at least sixteen, if not older. The boys fell into step with her quite happily, crossing over her little bridge without a mishap. And, when she got into her backyard, she led the way out to her front yard and then said, "There you go. That's my cul-de-sac. But I think you want the next cul-de-sac over. So you have to go down and around that way." And she gave them instructions regarding how to get to Penny's cul-de-sac, probably closer to the house where these teens came from. The young men smiled and thanked her; then they took off, walking in the direction she suggested. She smiled, and, as soon as they were out of sight, she turned back to Mugs and said, "Well, that was our good deed for the day."

He barked several times, but he didn't seem to be all that happy. She wished she'd taken pictures of the two boys. She had tried to identify some characteristics for each just because she wasn't comfortable dealing with strangers anymore, yet nothing had seemed to distinguish these teens. No tattoos. No piercings. No scars. No moles. No singular hairstyles or shocking stripes of color in their hair. Still, she jotted down a few notes on her cell phone and then turned and said, "Guys, it's bedtime. Let's get inside and crash for the night."

And that's what they did.

Chapter 5

Saturday Morning...

THE NEXT MORNING, instead of waking up energized and full of life, she woke up exhausted. She'd had terrible nightmares about this Bill/Brian/Bob Small guy, and she was too tired to even figure out what his proper name was. Putting the coffee on, she noted it was still early. But then, considering that Mack was supposed to start working with her on the deck, she needed to be feeling a little bit better. And she'd promised she would eat before he got here. Her animals looked like they'd had as rough a night as she had.

Mugs was stretched out flat on the floor, his legs almost in a weird little froggy position.

"What's with you today?" she asked, crouching down and rubbing him behind the ears. He yawned and rolled over, and she assumed it meant that his beauty sleep had been cut short. Thaddeus still snoozed on the back of a chair, and she saw absolutely no sign of Goliath. She figured he'd found a corner somewhere in the house and was busy pretending that nobody else had gotten up.

She sat by the coffeepot, desperately waiting for it to

finish so she could have her first cup. Did she even have food to eat? She looked in the fridge and was thankful she had enough to make an omelet. And a hefty-size one too. She pulled out the ingredients and started to get it ready but didn't want to until she had her first cup of caffeine. With that done and the first cup poured, she opened the back door and propped it ajar.

As she walked out, she smiled because this would be her last day with this tiny deck. Of course it could be worse. She might have no deck; she hadn't considered that because, before anybody could build a new deck, the old one had to come down first.

She sighed and said to Mugs, "The things you do to improve your life." He woofed a little but was basically telling her that he didn't give a darn. She could relate. She walked down to the creek with the animals, Goliath appearing out of nowhere and shooting right down to the creek ahead of her. Once there, she looked at the water but didn't think it was any higher. Yet from the wet ridge a little bit past where the water level was now, she noted it had gone higher during the night. She walked to check the hoses, and there, every once in a while, water gushed out.

"So the pumps are working," she said out loud. It also meant that the creek was that much higher and that the groundwater was soaking backward toward the house. But still, everything was doing what it needed to do. And, with that thought, she plunked her butt down on the grass and sighed. "I want to go back to sleep," she announced to the world. But, of course, nobody was listening.

She sat here for the longest moment, sipping her coffee and enjoying the fact that she had at least gotten up a little earlier, so she didn't have to deal with Mack right in her face for the moment. He'd be here soon enough. As long as she had a chance to get where she needed to be first, which mentally meant she needed to get her engines turned on, then she'd be fine. With the coffee, she sat for a little bit longer and then got up and walked back to the house.

As she walked in, Mack came around from the side of the house, entering her kitchen. She stopped, stared, and said, "You're early."

"I am," he said. "You look like crap."

She glared at him, and he shrugged, but she could see his grin slipping sideways. "Hey, I'm just saying."

"Well, if you're expecting any coffee, you better not be saying," she snapped.

He stopped, looked at her, and asked, "Any problem?"

She shook her head. "No," she said. "I'm just tired. I had a bad night."

"Good enough," he said. Then he went back out toward his truck. She followed.

He had dropped a bunch of stuff on the ground. "Is that all the stuff you bought last night?"

He nodded. "Make sure you eat," he said. "And make sure there's coffee for me too."

She groaned and nodded, then headed back inside and poured herself a second cup of coffee. She poured him one too and knew they would need a second pot anyway, so she put that on now. She then started to make herself a hefty omelet. When he clumped up the stairs ten minutes later and walked in with a couple flats of beer, she stared at the beer, then at him.

He looked at her omelet in appreciation. "Wow," he said. "You keep telling me that you're making omelets. I'm really glad to see that you're getting a little more creative."

"Maybe," she said, "but I don't know how to be creative. I don't really know what goes with what."

"Everything goes with anything, as long as you like it," he said.

She groaned. "I added zucchini to my sandwich yesterday."

He stopped, then looked at her and said, "Well, okay, maybe not that far."

She chuckled. "It wasn't that bad."

"It's just another vegetable," he said with a shrug. He walked over and picked up his cup of coffee, then took a sip of it. When it'd cooled enough, he took a bigger drink.

"Did you get all the shopping done last night?" she asked.

He nodded, walked over, dug into his pocket, and pulled out some bills and coins. "That's the change from the materials and the booze," he said.

She was surprised to see over $40 left. "Do you think you'll need more?"

He nodded. "Just leave that accessible," he said, "and we'll see what else we might have to get over the weekend."

"What we know for sure is that we'll need more stain," she said.

"Yep, so don't spend that in your mind."

"No," she said. "I won't. I'm wondering if we'll have enough for the rest of the deck without spending everything that was in the bowl."

"We'll give it a good try," he said.

As soon as she popped the last bite of omelet into her mouth, she stood and cleaned up the kitchen, then grabbed her gardening gloves and turned to him and asked, "How do we start?"

He grinned. "The best part," he said. "We take it all down."

"I was thinking about that this morning," she said. "That doesn't sound like much fun."

"It's actually great fun," he said cheerfully. "And most of it is rotten anyway."

"Is it?"

"It is." He took her out to the deck and said, "We'll make you a way to get up and down into your kitchen, but we have to take all this off."

She sighed. "What will keep up the little roof on the railing?" she asked.

He grinned and pointed to the long two-by-fours he had unloaded from his truck. "We'll prop it up here, and we'll do that part first."

As she watched, he grabbed the two-by-fours and made almost like a cross brace with four bars, propping them up underneath the little roof over the deck. And then he took a sledgehammer and knocked the railing out that was holding it up.

"Oh my," she said. There was a bit of a *ping*, but the roof itself didn't budge. She shook her head. "I wouldn't even have thought of that."

"Maybe not. None of this is salvageable. The wood's done," he said, showing her the cracks in the wood.

She nodded. "So, does all this railing and stuff go?"

"It all has to go," he said. "I thought we'd make a pile on the far side by the fence where the other materials are, but separate, so we can haul it out later."

She frowned as she thought about it and then pointed over by the shed. "But won't it have nails and stuff? If so, then let's put it over there, away from the driveway and the people traffic."

He nodded and said, "Good enough." And then he started grabbing wood and moving the old stuff over.

She stood and stared. "Am I supposed to knock this down then?" she asked.

"Sure." He came back with a sledgehammer in his hand and with two very light taps, the entire railing appeared to disintegrate. "Let's move this first," he said. "Then we'll start taking off the floorboards."

She quickly jumped in to grab little bits of railing, some of it still attached to the top of the railing, and the others basically dangling, and got it all carried over to the side. All three of the animals were outside with them, sitting close by and watching. When they returned to her deck, he said, "Now the steps."

She groaned and said, "I was hoping we could leave that to get in and out."

"Nope, not happening," he said. And, in two swipes, the steps were gone.

She stared and gasped. "Wow," she said. "What was holding all this together?"

"A prayer," he said jokingly. "It's a damn good thing we're doing it this weekend, as the bottom of the boards are all completely rotten."

"I could have fallen through at any time."

"Absolutely," he said. And, within half an hour, the entire deck structure and steps had all been hauled off to the side of her shed. She stood at the open space from the ground to her open kitchen door and smiled. "I can't quite jump up there," she said.

"You shouldn't try either," he said. He brought over three of the cinder blocks and plunked them down, one single one on its long side, then two atop each other behind that first one, so she could use those as temporary steps.

She smiled and said, "I can almost make that."

Just then a shout came from the front.

"Is that for me or for you?"

"Well, in this instance, I'd say both," he said with a big grin.

She raised her eyebrows. "What are you up to you?"

He shook his head and said, "You'll see."

She waited, and, all of a sudden, a group of men came around the corner. Arnold and Chester, Dan, Tommy, and even the captain. She stared at Mack in surprise. "Hey," she said. "Are you guys here to help?" she asked hopefully.

They all had big grins on their faces. "We figured we might owe you a little bit of assistance," the captain said, rubbing his hands together. "So, what are we building?"

After that, the entire group became this big happy family, but she hated to say it, with her on the outside. *Still.* Since she didn't know how to build a deck or what the procedure was or how to start, she kept finding herself in the way. Finally Mack, at one point in time, picked her up and plunked her on the cinder blocks at the doorstep and said, "Sit." She dropped her butt onto the kitchen threshold and glared at him. He smiled and said, "Let us figure this out first."

And, sure enough, all the other cinder blocks were set down in the backyard. They were having lots of discussions about how to measure and lay them, with Mack even changing a few of his plans, with the other guys making suggestions about how to maximize the boards if they made the deck a little bit longer and wider. And then not all the boards would have to be cut. She loved that idea, and they had ten-footers and eight-footers and, if they just rotated them, then maybe they wouldn't waste any of the wood. But what surprised her was the time frame required to get those cinder blocks down into the ground and then level. They had all kinds of stuff, from shovels to rakes, but nobody had mentioned the tarps.

"Mack?" she called out.

Distracted, he looked up to her and asked, "What?"

"Remember the tarps?" she asked anxiously.

He looked at her, down on the ground, and then nodded. "Where are they?"

She scrambled to her feet, then dashed inside to the kitchen and headed through to the garage. She returned a moment later with the two big tarps and handed them off. Mack grabbed them and opened them up, then gave her the packaging. And, with the men's help, they opened the tarps, spread them down, and used the corners of the cinder blocks to keep the edges anchored.

The guys heartily approved. "What's the matter? Don't you weed down here?" one of them teased.

"Not really," she said drily. "This will help slow them down a little bit."

"But you also have to consider," the captain said in that deep voice of his, "that these tarps will stop the rain from going into the ground."

She frowned at that. "So I'm not sure what's the best thing to do then," she said.

"Well, the tarp is great if you had a way for the water to go through it. But, if you don't, we'll need to punch some holes because you don't want the water sitting here and getting stagnant," he said.

"Agreed," she said, still frowning. "So let's figure this

out."

"We could if we had some coffee," Mack said.

She glared at him. "Is that your way of telling me to leave you alone?"

He chuckled, his laughter infectious, bright, and loud. Everybody stopped and stared at him.

Doreen figured it was to see how she took being laughed at. Mack was always teasing her. It was just not evident to these guys yet.

Mack shook his head. "If I thought getting you to make coffee would keep you out of trouble," he said, "we would have cheerfully delivered you coffee every day to have you butt out of our lives."

She promptly put her hands on her hips, then glared at him and said, "Mack Moreau. You behave yourself. I've been a big help."

"You have, indeed," he said. "You've also been a big pain in the butt."

At that, all the men laughed. She nodded and said, "Okay, you've got me there. Because of that, I'll go put on coffee."

And she dashed into her kitchen to put on coffee. Inside, she couldn't believe how great it was to have a neighborly visit like this, with everybody pitching in to help.

Chapter 6

Saturday Midafternoon ...

THE HOURS BLENDED into each other as Doreen did her best to help by bringing water and refilling coffee. She understood now what Mack had said about the hidden costs of having a group like this because the coffee disappeared pot after pot. She'd no sooner make a pot than she was emptying it and putting on another pot. By the time midafternoon had arrived, the men appeared extremely proud of themselves. She, for one, didn't have a clue what they had done to be proud of. All the cinder blocks were partly in the ground, and they had string lined up, and they were all standing around, looking mighty pleased. She looked at Mack and shrugged in question. He grinned back at her and said, "I put a dozen beers in the fridge. It'd be a really good time to bring them out now."

"Good timing because we just ran through, like, our eighteenth pot of coffee," she joked.

The men groaned. "Did you say beer? You mean, you had beer in there the whole time?" Arnold asked. "What are we doing drinking coffee then?" The guys joked and laughed back and forth, but it was obvious that they had a lot of respect for each other. She went into the kitchen, exchanged two room-temperature six-packs for the cold ones in her fridge, and brought them outside. Those disappeared almost immediately into greedy hands.

As they cracked open the tops and took their first drinks, she asked, "So could somebody explain what this was all about?" She gestured with her hands to the stringed-off area.

The captain stepped up and gave her a really clear understanding of why this foundational part of the new deck was so vital and why they'd spent the time that they did. The fact that they'd dug a drain underneath the tarps so all the water would go into the wells where the sump pumps were also amazed and surprised her. They'd left the tarps atop that added feature to slow the weeds. The captain continued, "You've got two sumps going on here, so we wanted to make sure that any of the water that came in through here would slip down toward the sump pumps." A pipe stuck out of the end of the ditch where they had dug down to meet up where the sump pumps were.

"Wow," she said, understanding the basic logic. "That's perfect." She was absolutely thrilled. "So what happens now?"

"Now we'll lift all those big timbers," Chester said, wiping his brow. He had a beer in his hand, and she almost wanted to ask if he was old enough to drink it. That was a compliment, but the kid looked sixteen. She didn't know why she hadn't noticed that before, but it was amazingly obvious now. A shout came from around the house, and Mack walked over there, then lifted a hand in greeting and turned back and said, "Now we're talking."

And additional guys came, whom she more or less recognized, and one of them was the guy from yesterday. He came, took one look at their progress so far, smiled, and said, "Hey, we came just at the right time."

"Didn't you though," Chester growled. "All the hard work is done."

The two men exchanged slaps on their shoulders, and everybody offered their greetings.

Mack held up his beer and said, "We have cold beer, if you want one."

The guys rubbed their hands together. "Perfect timing," one said. "We just arrived, and the beers are already out."

Doreen disappeared into the house and pulled out another six-pack, hoping it was cold enough. If she didn't have Mack's coaching, she wouldn't have a clue. Because, at her house with her husband, the butlers and caterers were always around to handle things like that. She understood filling somebody's wineglass and lifting flutes from a tray, but deciding when somebody would have a beer was something that she didn't get. She also wasn't so sure that beer was something she wanted to drink. It smelled awfully strong. She couldn't remember if she'd ever had one or not. It was a long way away from champagne.

The six-pack disappeared pretty quickly, and the new arrival mentioned something about pulling the deck a little farther out in order to have adequate space for people to sit and for a better alignment of the deck with the house. That started another heavy discussion. She sat here, wondering if anybody would ask her about it, but the thing was, she didn't really care because what she really wanted was a big deck and didn't care how far out or over it went. Mack was explaining about the side yards and putting something down, like landscape cloth and gravel or something, so that she could use that space to walk back and forth.

"You need gates though," the captain said. "You've got the dog and the cat. You need to gate that off on the side. Both sides actually. You know what? I think I've got a little gate back at the house. We could probably frame it up pretty fast." And that started more discussions.

The new guy said, "If you got any spare wood, I can build a gate for the other side. You're right that she needs to keep the dog and the cat in the backyard."

That made absolutely no sense to her when there was no gate or fence down to the creek. But then she did worry about the street in front of the house, and that was no issue at the back. Regardless, as long as the men were happy, who was she to argue? But, as she listened to the men's logic, she had to wonder. They were all having such fun being themselves. There was such a male-bonding thing going on.

Just then her phone rang. As the men talked, she looked to see it was Nan. Doreen grinned and answered the phone. "Hi, Nan."

"I hear voices. What are you up to?" Nan asked.

"Well, the guys are all here working on my deck," she said. "Can you hear them?" And she held her phone up so all the discussions filtered through.

Nan laughed. "Oh my," she said. "You've done well."

"I don't know about that," Doreen said, "but I might get a deck—at least I hope so because right now I have nothing. It's all been demolished."

Nan giggled like a little girl. "But, my dear, you've found the best thing ever. You've found help. You've got all those men to come help you."

"I don't think I got them to do anything," Doreen said, chuckling. "This is all Mack."

"All cops, isn't it?"

"Well, it was," she said cautiously, "but we've got some new people now too."

"That's all good," she said.

In the background, Doreen could hear Mack explaining about putting patio blocks all the way down to the creek and a bench down there. And the men had an even more heated discussion, but all apparently on good terms because she couldn't hear anybody getting upset or angry. She was amazed to hear everybody pitching an idea about how to fix up the entire backyard. She just wanted a huge patio and a big deck and a pathway to the creek, but that wouldn't be enough for these guys. No, it had to be stamped concrete and had to be this and had to be that. The only thing was, she didn't know if anybody except Mack understood just how dire her financial situation was.

At one point, Nan asked, "Are you listening to them or to me?"

"Honestly, Nan, it's hard to hear anything," she said.

"Good," Nan said. "Then I'll tell you real quick. The other lady didn't have a heart condition."

"Which lady was that?"

"Bella," she said. "She was the overweight one. She did have a heart murmur, and the one, Kimmy, did have a heart condition, but the other one, Delilah, did not. But she still keeled over as if she did have a heart attack."

"I suppose that could happen, at her age maybe," Doreen said cautiously, her mind distracted as she thought about the three women. And the kiwis …

"Maybe," Nan said. "But believe me, Delilah's family thinks it's very suspicious."

"Why is that?"

"Because she just changed her will. I overheard her talking to Rosie about it at Rosemoor."

At any mention of money, Doreen's ears perked up. "For or against the family?"

"I knew you'd ask that," Nan said, chuckling. "She cut out her nephew."

"Oh, dear," she said. "But then, that would be a little too obvious."

"But still, if he wanted revenge, that's a good way to get it."

"But, in another six months, he could have made it so that he was back in Delilah's good graces," Doreen said.

"Oh, I didn't think about that," Nan said. "Well, I'll keep digging." And she hung up.

Doreen put away her phone, slowly wishing all the cops would now start talking about these cases. But she got up and hopped into the kitchen instead, then quickly wrote down notes in her laptop of what Nan had just said. As Doreen was just about done, she heard somebody walking toward her. All of a sudden, Mack filled the kitchen doorway. She looked up guiltily and slammed down the lid. He stared at her laptop, looked at her, and narrowed his gaze. She gave him the sweetest smile she could muster. "How's all the beer holding up?"

"The beer's doing fine," he said. "We've got a few ideas we want to run past you."

"And here I thought you guys were making decisions all on your own," she teased.

He chuckled and said, "No, we're definitely asking you. That doesn't mean you'll want to hear everything we say beforehand, to reach a consensus."

"It's the price tag that bothers me," she muttered, as she headed out with him. Then was distracted by the captain, holding a gate. She looked at it and smiled. "Where'd you get that from so quickly?"

"My wife just brought it," he said. "And a can of black metal spray paint. I was thinking that maybe you'd like a little gate along the side here. Obviously we can't put it in place while all this material's being moved, but it would fit right up at the front by the house." And he motioned her to follow him so she could see what he meant.

"It would look great," she said. "How would we attach it?"

"That's no problem," he said. "We can construct a frame for it and have it open and shut. Maybe this direction." But, as he swung it, he said, "You know what? I think this one can open both ways."

"Can we latch it?"

And he opened his other hand to show her the metal latch and said, "My wife brought that too."

"Perfect," she said in delight. "That's really kind of her."

"I don't know about it being kind of her," he said, "as much as it's something I was supposed to clean up months ago." His voice was sheepish, as if to say he'd been in trouble over the whole deal.

Doreen chuckled. "Hey, that works for me too," she said. "Much appreciated."

"Not a problem," he said. "We've got the rest of this to get on with, but some of us can be working on this too."

"That's perfect," she said with a big fat smile.

As they headed over to the rest of the men, Mack called her toward the edge of the deck location. "Either we can put steps down toward Richard's place or we can do steps all the way around," he said. "Or we put up railings."

She frowned. "Right. We're back to that railing thing,

aren't we?" she said. "What are the pros and cons?"

Immediately the men jumped in with comments. "Well, if you put a railing up, you can put chairs closer to the edge. No danger of falling over."

"Wow," she said. "I didn't even think about that." She contemplated the edge of her new deck and how high off the ground it would be. "And that is a problem even if steps are all the way around, isn't it?"

"Particularly if you want to put a barbecue or a table and chairs up here," the new arrival said. "My suggestion was to bring the deck out a little bit farther and widen this section off. We'd have to add another couple cinder blocks, but that's it. And you've got some spares. You could have steps that go down here, and we could put a railing up on this side and leave the front wide open with the steps. That would allow you lots of places to sit, and you can put all kinds of furniture up here, and then you'll have a stairway all across this long deck side facing the creek. And a short narrow set of stairs going from the deck down toward Richard's fence, so you can easily go down to that side of the house."

She stared, noting the new markers for this version of the deck, and asked, "Do we have enough material for that though?"

Mack shook his head. "No, we don't," he said. "You'll be short a little bit, but I don't think it'll be too bad."

And she looked beyond the deck expansion and asked, "We're putting a patio in here, weren't we?"

"And we still can," he said, "but we'll start it from this side and pour it in that direction." He talked about a four-foot concrete patio from where the deck steps went across the one edge of the deck and then all the way down and into a big patio section.

"Well, that would look quite nice," she said in surprise. "Anyway, are you making the patio and this sidewalk here run all the way down to the creek?"

"It can go down a way, then also go all around the side of the house," the new guy said. "Up to this side." He pointed it all out. "You could even put stamped concrete all the way down both sides."

"I would love to have all this area cleaned up into stamped concrete," she admitted but hating to feel the money issue rear it's ugly head, "but that sounds very expensive."

The men frowned as they muttered about cost and framing and whatnot. "You can't do it all at once today," the new guy said. She couldn't even remember his name. "But, if we can get it framed up, it's pretty cheap to get the bags of concrete and mix yourself."

"That's a lot to pour though," the captain said. "It would all have to be done pretty fast."

"And I can't afford to bring in a truck," she said.

"You know what? I don't think it would take all that long," said Tony, the newest guy. "I got a little mixer, and that's pretty easy. We could do all this little sidewalk area probably in one single pour. And, while it's being leveled, we could be mixing up another batch to go along here."

Nobody else had any experience with concrete, just him, so he said, "Let me go home and take a look at what I've got and how it might work out. You guys get working on the deck, and I'll come back with some deck boards that I've still got there." Then he paused before continuing, "I think I have some railing as well. I might have enough to do that one side." And, with that, he took off.

She looked around at the others and said, "I hate to keep

you all on a weekend. This is a good time to stop for the day."

The men immediately shook their heads. "If we're widening and lengthening the deck, let's get the beams down on the cinder blocks on the other side, then we'll add in the big crossbeams."

She sighed, shrugged, and watched. She walked over to Mack, who was busy talking to the captain. She tapped him gently on the arm. He looked down at her, smiled, and asked, "What do you think?"

"I think all of them are great ideas," she said. "I'm worried about a small project going big."

"Yes," he said, "but keep in mind what your original budget was too."

She nodded. Then, in a whisper, she said, "What about pizza?"

Chapter 7

Saturday Early Evening ...

MACK NODDED AND looked at the captain. "How long will you be around?"

The captain looked at his watch and said, "Oh, I'm good for a couple more hours. Did I hear you say pizza?" And a big grin crossed his face as he patted his tummy. "I can only get pizza when my wife is not around," he said. "Otherwise, you know what that's like."

Mack chuckled. Several of the other guys turned, looked, and said, "Did you say pizza?"

"Well, I was thinking I should probably order some," she said. "You guys are working so hard."

"You can always order in pizza," one of the guys said. "But good luck trying to get us to agree on what kinds."

"Is that really a problem?" she asked. "Here I was figuring I could buy a couple of the most common varieties, like supreme pepperoni and say, you know, ham and pineapple or something."

All the men were nodding. "You know what? That works," Arnold said.

Mack looked down at her. And then he whispered,

"How would you know what the most common varieties are?"

She beamed up at him. "Internet," she said. "It gives us all kinds of good ideas. So, six?" But her voice was hesitant. "Are you guys eating one each?"

Arnold nodded, but Chester shook his head. Arnold immediately sacked him in the gut and said, "Of course you are."

Chester rolled his eyes. "You are too funny," he said. "If you eat too much pizza, I'll tell your wife." At that, the two of them wrangled about it.

She chuckled, looked up at Mack, and said, "What's your best guess?"

"Get seven just to make sure," he said.

She nodded and headed back inside. She'd never ordered pizza in her life. So she took her phone to her laptop, with a web page already up. One was supposed to order online, but that didn't look like something she wanted to do. So she called them.

When she explained what she was looking for, the guy on the other end laughed and said, "Not a problem. We can get it to you in about thirty minutes." She was delighted with that. He also said that she could pay cash when the pizza got there. When she got word of the bill, her eyes rounded.

"Sure," she said in a strangled voice. "That sounds good." She would also have to add a tip. With the total pizza bill, she grabbed her wallet and carefully counted out the money, including a tip. She didn't want to disturb the guys as long as they were working, so she'd wait for the pizzas, when it was time to eat. Then they could be completely sidetracked with that. As she refilled her fridge with more beers, she decided to stay in her kitchen, out of the way.

Mack hopped inside, looking for another beer.

She said, "Pizza is on the way."

"Good," he said.

She stepped forward, closer, and said, "Do you think I can afford all these new changes?"

"Yep," he said. "We're getting there. We might still need to buy some things, but it shouldn't be too bad."

"I hope so," she said. "You know how broke I am."

"I know," he said, "but think of this in another way. You're adding a ton of value to your home. More than that, you'll have so much joy having your deck and a patio. The patio was a really good idea."

"How much would it be to get a truck in to pour that?" she asked.

He frowned. "If it's all ready to go, and you have somebody who can actually work it, it's still likely to be about $1,000 to $1,500."

She sucked in her breath at that.

He nodded. "But remember…"

She interrupted him. "I know. I know," she said. "We were planning on paying at least that anyway to begin with."

"It's hard to spend money," he said sympathetically.

"It's hard to spend money you don't have," she said. "The pizzas will be about $90."

He nodded. "And don't forget we might repeat this tomorrow."

She nodded. "Right. Good thing I had that bowl of money from Nan."

"Do you still have the cash?" he asked. "Just in case."

"Yes," she said. "I didn't move it."

"Good," he said. And, with that, he hopped back out

again. She stood here and watched from the kitchen as the men worked. She made some iced tea and, after pouring herself a glass, put it into the fridge. Hearing a sound, she walked to the front door. And, sure enough, a pizza guy walked toward her steps with a huge stack of pizzas. She opened the door as he reached the bottom of the steps, and she laughed at him. "Wow," she said. "That's a big stack."

He grinned and said, "Well, it sounds like you've got a crew working in the backyard."

"I do," she said. She held out her hands to take the seven pizzas.

"Show me where the kitchen is, and I can take this directly in," he said. "You don't want to be carrying them. They're hot."

She opened the door wider and led the way to the kitchen table, and he dropped them there for her. "Here's the money, with a tip for you for delivering it too. Thank you for that."

As he accepted the money, he took one look at the crew and said, "Wow. I'm out of here. That's all cops."

She chuckled. "Yep, sure are." As soon as he was gone, she shut the front door and headed to the kitchen. She picked up two different pizzas and carried them out to the back. "I don't have an outside table big enough for all you guys," she said. "So I'll open these and offer whoever wants one."

The first pizza was pepperoni, and everybody had one piece, and it was soon gone. She shook her head, opened the supreme, and said, "This one's got everything." And everybody had a piece of that too. But now they each had one they were eating and one they were holding, and she already had two empty pizza boxes. She grabbed the ham and pineapple and held it out. "So, now that you guys are all full, I can have this one, right?" she teased.

But Chester was already out of pizza.

"Are you empty-handed already?" she asked. He nodded and grabbed the largest piece in the box. She took this moment to grab a piece for herself, and it was hot and gooey and delicious. She moaned. "I can't remember the last time I had a good pizza."

"About six weeks ago," Mack said, "when I delivered it."

"I remember that." He was also out of pizza. She walked over with the box in her hand, and he took another slice. By the time he had his, several more guys had reached for another one. And this pizza was gone. She now had three empty boxes. When her piece was gone, she made her way into the kitchen and opened another and offered it one-handed to the guys. And she did the same for the pepperoni that was next, and very quickly she had distributed enough pizza that a few slices remained in the box, while the guys were still eating. She looked at Mack and asked, "More beer?"

He nodded, walked to the kitchen, and brought out two more six-packs. Everybody got another beer, and they sat on cinder blocks or the ground, drinking beer and eating pizza. By the time she had six empty boxes, she was stunned. "Well, you guys eat a lot."

"Is the pizza gone?" Chester asked.

"Nope," she said. "I did order a seventh." He grinned as she made her way over, climbed up the lovely cinder block steps into her kitchen, and brought out the last box. "If you guys eat more than this, you're pigs."

Immediately they all made snorting sounds of a piglet. But still, only two of them needed another piece, while the others held up their hands and said, "No, we're good."

"Yay. If you leave me some, I will have it for breakfast," she said mockingly.

Immediately Chester looked at the piece in his hand.

"She was joking," Mack called out.

"Eat," she said. "I'm happy to feed anybody who's working to build me a deck."

He grinned and said, "That's the way of it. It's always best to have beer and pizza with a gang like this."

She nodded. "Love the camaraderie," she said. "Nice to know that you guys don't hate each other after working together all the time."

And with Chester being the only one still eating, the others headed back to work. She could see it was a much slower job now, but they had the other blocks dug in for the expansion that they had talked about. And, with a plan, they got started, and, before long, they had a frame with metal hangers in position, supporting some of the crossbeams. It looked lovely, even though she knew they were less than half done. With that accomplished, a couple of them said they had to leave.

She nodded and said, "Thank you very much."

Four of them weren't coming back the next day apparently, according to Mack, as he stood there beside them, saying goodbye. But the others would.

She smiled and waved, and after about an hour, the rest of the men had all trickled away. It was past 7:30 p.m. already and heading closer to 8:00. "Wow," she said, letting out a long and slow breath. "It's been a long day."

"A very long day," he said with a smile, "but a good day."

"Are we likely to get much more done tomorrow?"

"Yeah," he said. "Especially now that we have some extra hands, it should be good."

"But most of the hands aren't coming back tomorrow."

"Well, they're not coming back first thing," he said, "but I have a few other guys who might show up."

"You've got enough beer for tomorrow?"

He chuckled. "I do," he said. "You got enough pizza?"

She shook her head. "No way do I have enough pizza for another gang." She laughed. "But I can get more."

Chapter 8

Sunday Morning ...

THE NEXT MORNING, Doreen woke up slowly, dragging her body from bed. She was sore in places she didn't even know it was possible to be sore. And that confounded her because, well, she hadn't done any of the physical work accomplished yesterday. She'd had a shower before going to bed the previous night, which didn't work out so well right now. A nice hot shower might work out the soreness in her muscles. But she didn't think she had time and knew she would need some coffee and food before her day started.

As she checked her watch, she was surprised to realize it was already eight. She hadn't talked to Mack about what time they would all be arriving to work on the deck but figured it would be soon.

Dressing quickly, she headed down to put on the coffeepot. And then she stepped outside, carefully making her way down her temporary steps that they had put in place so she could get in and out of the kitchen. Although a lot had been done yesterday, still a lot was left to be done today. As they had gotten the foundational crossbeams lined up, one of the guys had started laying down some of the decking boards.

But that hadn't lasted, and he did it more to ensure that it would look good. And honestly, from where she stood, it would look dynamite. But no way to know until it was all done.

It still amazed her just how much didn't get done, and yet how much, according to Mack, had been done. She figured that maybe the deck could have been done in one day, but then, with all the measuring and leveling and brainstorming, that had been too high an expectation. And what did she know? She had no experience in this stuff.

When the coffee was done dripping, she yawned, poured herself a cup, and then stepped back outside again, making her way carefully to the edge of the lawn. She should have gone through the garage. It would have been easier. She walked down to the creek, rotating her neck and lifting and shrugging her shoulders, trying to ease some of the stiffness there. The animals appeared to be just as exhausted as she was. She looked down at Mugs and said, "It's nice having the company, isn't it?"

But he didn't even bother giving her a growl or a bark. He grumbled a little bit and carried on with his head down, plodding forward. She appreciated that. That was something she could relate to, her head down and plodding forward, even if she didn't like what was coming at her. Life still had to be tackled one way or another.

At the water, she sat down on the grass carefully, groaning as her butt hit the softer ground, and yet it still wasn't soft enough. As she looked up at the clouds, she decided none of the clouds would be soft enough either. Who knew her butt could hurt like this? It must have been all the bending and crouching that she'd done, taxing her glutes. Maybe her temporary steps that forced her into those deeper movements with her legs. At least that sounded plausible. She sat here quietly in a half doze, her eyes drifting shut, sipping away at her coffee. When her phone rang, she looked to see it was Mack. "Good morning, Mack," she said, trying hard to eject some energy into her voice.

But he was distracted. "Change of plans," he said abruptly.

"Oh, what change?" she asked, shifting to look around at her nonexistent deck in progress.

"We found another body," he said.

"Another gray-haired lady?" She bounced to her feet, spilling the last of her coffee on the ground. She groaned.

"What's the matter?" he asked.

"I'm down at the creek," she said, "and I accidentally spilled my coffee."

His voice lightened at that. "I wish I had coffee," he said. "None of us will arrive anytime soon."

"Oh," she said. "Well then."

"Sorry," he said, "but, in this case, we're all hands on deck. Although a couple guys might show up. You'll have to explain to them what's going on."

"Sure," she said. "I guess no finished deck till next weekend then, huh?"

"I'm sorry," he said. "I'm afraid not."

And she heard true regret in his voice. She stood with a smile, although the disappointment was crushing. "That's all right," she said. "It is what it is."

"Maybe, but it's hard to say if anybody will come this afternoon. I'll be here for hours, then forensics will step in, and I can get away for a little bit," he said. "I'll stop by when and if I can and see if anybody is there."

"But the only people who would be here are ones who

weren't called in, right?"

"Right," he said. "But I think Tony might have been coming anyway."

"Which one is Tony?" she asked.

"He's the one who brought the last of the boards and is the concrete guy."

"Wow," she said. "Nothing he can do, is there?"

"Not likely," Mack said, "but you could always talk to him about what you want and the cost involved."

"I can do that," she said. "Is everything measured out so Tony knows where the stairs stop? If we did want to frame up for the concrete patio?"

"Yep," Mack said. "We already did that stuff yesterday and talked to him about it."

"Wasn't he seeing what he had at home?"

"Yeah, but then his mom fell," Mack said. He stopped and said, "Didn't I tell you that?"

"No," she said. "You didn't. I'm sorry to hear that. I hope she's okay."

"She was already at the hospital when she fell, so at least she was getting the care she needed on the spot."

"How did she fall then?"

"She was walking down the hall and caught her foot in her walker apparently," he said. But, once again, Mack's tone was distracted.

"Sounds terrible," she said. "If I see him, I'll talk to him. Otherwise I'll see you when you get here."

"Good enough," he said, and he hung up.

She looked down at Mugs. "Well, it's not exactly what we had hoped for," she said. "But, considering we got what we did already, maybe it's not the worst thing that could have happened." She knew a lot more than just decking boards had to go down. She wasn't sure exactly what though. And it was well beyond her to make those decisions. And then, as she walked back and took a closer look, she noted that the decking boards weren't screwed down. They'd only been laid in place for people to take a look. She nodded. "Right. So, another day. Another whole day. Particularly if we were doing railings." She groaned and made her way around to the garage, but it was locked from the inside, and she couldn't get in that way.

With difficulty, her butt screaming, she managed to get into the kitchen. And, for the animals, it was even harder. Well, Mugs tried and fell, so she had to get back outside and lift him up into the kitchen. Goliath managed with no trouble, and Thaddeus looked at it with that *poor me* look, so she picked him up also. "Just for a little while," she said to him gently.

He clicked several times and laid his head against hers. She smiled. "At least we get a slower morning."

In the kitchen, she remembered the leftover pizza. She opened the fridge to see the last three pieces from yesterday. Not even Chester finished it. When Mack had handed her those, he had said, "There you go. Breakfast."

As she stared at them, she wanted all three. All to herself, all three, right now.

Chuckling, she put them in the microwave to warm them up, knowing that Mack would tell her to put them in the little toaster oven because it warmed the crust better. With her pizza and a second cup of coffee, she went out the front door and sat on the steps there. She ate slowly, giving Mugs a couple small bites. Goliath took one sniff and ran off, as if offended. Thaddeus, on the other hand, eyed the green peppers with an overzealous look. She pulled one off the top and gave it to him. He ate about half and left it.

"That good, huh?"

He gave a weird shake of his head as if agreeing with her. She got up when she was done and went in, then cleaned up her kitchen, which hardly had anything dirty, considering the pizza was in a box. But she took that out to the recycling to see the other six pizza boxes in there, realizing how much fun the garbage people would have if they could see the contents of her container right now.

With the cleanup done, she went to her laptop. Chances were there wouldn't be any news on this latest death of another elderly lady. Doreen sat here, and her phone rang again. Expecting it to be Mack, she was surprised to see Nan calling. "Hey, Nan," she said, trying for a cheerful voice.

"Have you heard?" Nan asked, her voice broken.

"Heard what?" Doreen asked gently.

"It's," she said on a wail, "Rosie McDougal."

"What happened to Rosie?" Doreen asked. But in her heart she knew. "Has she passed away?"

"She died of a heart attack."

Doreen frowned. "Where?"

"Out on the path heading toward the manor," she said. "She lives here at Rosemoor, but, for some reason, she left the home and headed up the creek."

"And then she dropped dead from a heart attack?" Doreen asked, making sure she understood what was going on.

"Yes," Nan wailed. "She was the sweetest thing. She was always handing out kiwis to everyone. She wasn't part of that clique thing, and I think she did it kind of tongue-in-cheek because she was after the coveted award this year."

Kiwis? Award? Uh-oh. "Did she have a heart condition?"

"Only because of that grandson of hers," Nan said in a foreboding voice. "He was always so mean to her and was trying to get money off her, leaving her in tears."

"But that doesn't mean she had a heart condition," Doreen said. "Would anybody expect her to die from a heart attack?"

"Oh, no, no, no," Nan said. "Her blood pressure was fine. She was really good after her last cancer checkup, and she was free and clear. Nobody would have thought a heart attack would take her."

"And do you know for sure it was her heart?" Doreen asked.

"Well, she dropped dead like all the others. You have to help," Nan cried out. "Doreen, this will take your special touch."

At that, Doreen's eyebrows shot up. "Nan, this is a current case. You know how the police will feel if I interfere."

"I don't care," Nan said mutinously. "This is Rosie. She wouldn't hurt a fly."

"That doesn't mean that she didn't fall or wasn't lying there for a long time in shock, and maybe fear sent her heart into overdrive, and she naturally collapsed and died," Doreen said gently. "I know it looks like the other cases, but, until the police have a chance to investigate, we won't know."

"No, you mean, they won't tell us," Nan said. Her tone was definitely upset.

"I get what you're saying," she said. "I know Mack is there now. I'm walking outside and down to the creek, heading toward you. So tell me what you know as I walk there." After taping a note for Tony on her kitchen door, in case he came while she was gone, she set up the alarms then left through the back yard. With her animals beside her, they walked all the way around and headed down to the path.

"Weren't they all supposed to be at your house today?" Nan asked.

"They were," Doreen said. "At least they were working on the house yesterday. But this death has called in a bunch of them."

"Of course it has," Nan said. "So whoever did this should pay twice."

Doreen shook her head. "My deck is hardly a priority now," she said.

"Well, it should be," Nan said. "Just think about it. I mean, if they weren't on this case, they would be helping get your deck finished."

"Sure, but it's more important that this lady is looked after."

"And that's why you're a very special woman," Nan said, her voice warming up nicely. "You'll get to the bottom of this, won't you?"

"Well, I can try, Nan. But you also know that it's not a cold case," she said.

"But what if it is made into a cold case?" Nan said excitedly. "Then Mack couldn't keep you out of it."

"Oh, of course he could," Doreen said. "Just think how much Mack tries to keep me out of things."

"Yes, but it doesn't always work that way," Nan said, thrilled. "Let me see if there's any mystery in Rosie's life, and I'll get back to you." And, with that, her phone went *snick*.

Doreen stared down at her phone and groaned. "I knew it was bound to happen sooner or later, but I didn't really want it to be today."

Just then the foursome reached the corner and neared Rosemoor. As she turned to look toward Nan's direction, sure enough, Doreen saw a group of policemen. She wandered toward her grandmother's apartment, knowing that Mack would see her soon enough. And he did. He stood and glared at her. She shrugged. "I really don't have any choice. Nan called me."

"What's Nan got to do with this?" he asked.

"Rosie McDougal is a friend of hers."

"And how did she know what happened?" he asked suspiciously.

Doreen rolled her eyes at him. "Come on, Mack. Remember the grapevine here. She already knew. She called me, and she sent me down here to make sure you guys understood that Rosie doesn't have a heart condition and that she wouldn't have dropped dead from a heart attack."

At that, one of the other guys looked up, and he stared at her.

She smiled. "Hey, Arnold."

"She doesn't have a heart condition?" he asked, scratching his head. "Because she sure looks like the others."

Doreen shook her head, her gaze on the sheet-covered body and its surroundings. Not a kiwi in sight. Interesting. "Apparently not. And she was diagnosed as cancer-free a year or so ago. Any sign of kiwis with her?"

"That's a darn shame," Arnold said, looking down at the body. "And there's one in her pocket. It's the darndest thing."

"Arnold ..." Mack warned, sending her a glare.

"However," she said, with a beaming smile in his direction, "there is a suspicious grandson in the mix."

"And why is that?" Mack asked.

"He's always bugging Rosie for money and leaves her in tears every time."

"Well, it's possible somebody might have wanted to off her early," said another voice behind Mack, straightening up as he had been crouched by the fence.

She looked at Chester and grinned. "Chester, how can you walk after all that pizza yesterday?"

He smirked back at her. "Is there more?"

She smacked her lips and shook her head. "I ate all three leftover pieces for breakfast. You'd be proud of me."

"Hey, that's pretty good for you," Chester said. "I must admit that pizza for breakfast is pretty easy to get down."

She chuckled and then looked down at the poor woman covered by the sheet. "I feel sorry for her and her family, if there is anybody besides the grandson. If it is the grandson, I'm hoping he doesn't inherit anything."

"Maybe not," Mack said, "but we don't know that anything is suspicious about this either."

She snorted. "When four little old ladies drop dead the same way, that's suspicious. Then there's the whole kiwi issue," she said. He glared at her, and she raised both hands in frustration. "I know. I know. It's not a cold case," she said. "But you know Nan won't leave me alone about this."

"You're not allowed to interfere," he said with a glare and a warning.

She gave him an innocent look. "Of course not," she said. "What could I possibly do to interfere? You've got this, Mack. You'll find who did this in a couple days."

"How do you figure that?" he asked.

"Because, once the media gets ahold of this," she said, "the pressure will be incredibly intense. It doesn't take me to tell you that four recent deaths of little gray-haired ladies is very suspicious."

"Maybe it was just their time," Arnold suggested.

"Sure. All outside and all in public, not one of them at home baking cookies?" she said. A frown crossed his face at that, and he reached up to scratch his head as he looked down at the lady. "It's also rather early in the morning for a woman who doesn't like walking," Doreen said.

"Nan's words of wisdom again, I presume," Mack said.

"Yes," she said. "Rosie doesn't like to walk anywhere, and I have no idea what she'd be doing on this pathway right now."

"I do," Mack said with a sorry sigh. He reached down with his gloved hands and pulled out an envelope tucked into the old lady's jacket pocket. On the outside was Doreen's name. "She was coming to you."

Chapter 9

Sunday Midmorning...

DOREEN STARED AT the envelope with her heart sinking. "Oh my," she said. "That poor woman." She shook her head in dismay. "Why did I oversleep?" she asked. "I could have been down here earlier. Maybe I'd have seen her."

"Well, she hasn't been gone very long," Arnold said. "We only got the phone call around eight."

"And I think there are rules about when they're allowed to leave the manor," she said, frowning. "Nan could tell me more about that." She looked at the envelope, then at Mack. "Have you opened it?"

"I'm proud of you," he said. "You didn't even ask for it."

"There's no point," she said. "You won't let me have it until the investigation is over."

"Exactly," he said, "it's my investigation."

She rolled her eyes. "So open it and let me know what she said. It'd probably give you pointers as to who might have done this to her."

Immediately all the others crowded around. Mack carefully opened the envelope, which wasn't sealed, and pulled out a little note. He read out loud, "Hi, Doreen. I'm a friend of your grandmother's. I'm a little worried about talking to you in person, so I'll leave you this note. Is there anything you can do about my grandson, Danny? He wants me to die, and he wants me to die early." There was almost a pout left in the air with that. "He says he has no money, and he needs mine, and I should die sooner than later. I'd really appreciate your help. Thanks, Rosie." Everybody stepped back with hard looks on their faces.

"It's a little too pat," Doreen said.

Mack looked at her and gave her a clipped nod. "Thank you," he said. "I was thinking the same thing."

"Meaning that the grandson didn't do it?" Arnold asked in confusion. "Why? He's a perfect suspect for this."

"Yes, that's quite true," she said, "but why the other dead older ladies then?"

"Ah," Arnold said with a nod. "It's one thing if it was just her, but it would be something else now that we've got four of them."

"Exactly," she said. "And I understand that one of the others had a heart condition and one definitely didn't. And I can't remember what Nan said about the third one."

"We'll find out," Mack said, as he returned the note to the envelope. He put it into an evidence bag and sealed it up.

She looked at it and said, "If and when there's an opportunity, any chance I could get a copy of that?"

"Why?"

"For my own sake," she said. "I'm really sorry I couldn't help her before she died. On the other hand," she said, slowly looking at the letter in the bag. "Do you have any handwriting to match it to? Because, if somebody hated the grandson, what a perfect way to start tying these murders on

KILLER IN THE KIWIS

him."

Chester grinned. "I like the way she thinks. She's devious."

"She's also not a cop," Mack said, handing the envelope off to Chester. "Make sure this gets tagged and processed."

Immediately Chester headed to the side, where he filled out the forensic form for chain of custody. She watched as they continued their investigation and then saw two men come around the corner. "Ah, the coroner is here," she said, backing up slightly.

"Yeah, why don't you go home now," Mack said. "I told you that I'd be up there sooner or later."

She rolled her eyes and said, "Good point. I'll go back and have coffee." She called the animals and headed toward home. She stopped at the creek on a nearby corner and sat down on a rock and watched them from a distance. She wasn't sure how they would treat this latest death, but it wouldn't take much to see that this was connected. And, even if all four deaths *weren't* connected, she hoped due diligence was done because, as soon as the cops left, she would go down and do the same thing. She called Nan and said, "I've just come from the crime scene."

Nan immediately gasped in joy. "I knew you could do it," she said.

"Well, your friend was coming to visit me," Doreen said. "At least she was planning on placing a letter on my back step or some way that I would find it." She quickly told Nan what the letter said.

"Oh, that's so like Rosie," she said. "She's so nonconfrontational, and she doesn't want to cause trouble for anybody."

"But her grandson was obviously causing trouble for

her."

"Yes," Nan said. "And it's really sad because she didn't have much money either."

"So, why would the grandson think that she did?"

"I don't know," Nan said. "The problem is the grandson knew that she used to have money, but she has since lost most of it."

"How did she lose it?"

"Stocks, bonds, and then, of course, her own son was a bit of a layabout too, so she was always bailing him out of this and that. But she lost him in a freak car accident. He's been gone a good fifteen or so years now."

"And so Rosie's grandson is the next layabout?"

"Unfortunately, yes. The apple didn't fall far from the tree."

"What was Rosie's husband like?"

"Pretty well the same."

"Poor Rosie. She's had a lot of problems in her life. What kind of a man was her husband?"

"David was a gambler," Nan said. "He loved to do anything but actual work. He figured it was all too good for him. He did consider himself a fancy-dancy gardener though."

"A gardener?" Doreen said. "That's a lot of work for a layabout."

"Well, for a long time, they had gardeners," Nan said, her tone turning hoity-toity. "You know what I mean."

Doreen rolled her eyes. "Sure, I know what you mean," she said, "but that doesn't make it the same thing. Heidi had money, but she still did a lot of her own gardening."

"Well, I think David was the same," she said. "Anyway, he went missing quite a few years ago, maybe ten years now."

"What do you mean, *missing*?" Doreen asked.

Nan gasped. "There you go!" she said. "There's your cold case. That's your *in* into this investigation! I forgot about that."

"What are you forgetting about?" Doreen cried out in frustration. "Nan, are you saying that Rosie's husband disappeared a decade ago?"

"Well, he was here one day and gone the next, and poor Rosie was beside herself. She had just been given her first diagnosis of breast cancer, I think," Nan said. "And, after that, it was really tough on her because her husband never showed up again."

"Well, if he's a louse, maybe having a wife who could be terminally ill sounded like too much work."

"I wouldn't put it past him," Nan said in a decisive tone of voice. "He really wasn't a good man."

"And was he ever declared dead?"

"I don't know," Nan said thoughtfully. "For all I know, Rosie might have divorced him and never told anybody."

"Well, if she wanted to save face, it's possible. Or, if he took up with a much younger woman, it's also possible," Doreen said, thinking of her own history.

"How sad is that, huh? She was with her husband for a good forty-plus years, and then she gets terminally ill like that, and he just ups and walks away."

"But was her diagnosis then terminal? Because obviously she lived another ten years."

"It might have been closer to eleven by now," Nan said, "because she's done two five-year sets where she's cancer-free."

"Which is why her death this morning," Doreen said with a nod, "is so much harder. She was still cancer-free and could have lived another ten to fifteen years."

"Exactly," Nan said. "She was only about seventy-four, I think."

"Interesting," Doreen said. "So, old enough to have had a heart attack but young enough to have still possibly lived even another twenty-five years."

"Exactly," Nan said. "We really should have a talk with that grandson."

"Somebody, likely Mack, will do the next-of-kin notification. If not, I'm sure he'll interview the grandson based on her letter alone," Doreen said. "Do you know who her lawyer was?"

"No, I'm not sure I do," she said. "I remember recommending somebody a few years ago. I don't know if she followed through or not."

"Well, because, otherwise, the grandson might get her estate."

"She was taking care of business a few days ago," Nan said. "I should have asked her then if there was a reason. But, you know, a lot of us are constantly trying to put things into order so that we can get free and clear in our own mind about what our wishes are when the time comes, so we're not leaving a headache for our heirs."

"Right," Doreen said drily. "I don't think most of them do what you did though."

"Oh my. You have no idea what I even have now," she said, chuckling. "There's a safety deposit box somewhere that's got all kinds of stuff in it."

Doreen stiffened. "What do you mean, *all kinds of stuff in it?*"

"Yeah, all kinds of stuff," Nan said cheerfully. "Anything I thought I could use or should keep over the years is in it."

"Like what, Nan?"

"Well, that's why it's in a safety deposit box," Nan said, "so I don't forget it. How can I possibly remember what's in there? So, don't ask." Another crazy rabbit hole with Nan.

Doreen took a slow, calming breath and asked, "Do you have the key to the safety deposit box?"

"I think so," she said. "Or I left it at the house. Did you find some keys in those pockets and the cupboards and the drawers when you were sorting through things?"

"Yes, I think there were keys," she said. "I didn't think any of them were for a safety deposit box though."

"Well, maybe I have it here still," she said. "I'm never too far from it."

"Well, Nan, if it's still in the house, you're quite far away from it," Doreen said gently.

"Oh, that's okay," she said. "Nobody will care about all that stuff in there anyway, at least not until I'm gone."

"Is it damaging information?" Doreen asked slowly. She hadn't a clue what her Nan was up to.

"Well, for some people it probably is," Nan said with certainty. "I did have fun over the years collecting stuff."

"Are there any valuables in it?"

"Not that one," Nan said. "The other one has valuables."

Doreen reached up and pinched the bridge of her nose. "Nan, are you saying you have two safety deposit boxes?"

"Yep, I sure do," she said. "Maybe more. I'll look. I did write all that stuff down. I showed it to you, didn't I?"

"No, I don't think so," Doreen said. "I don't think you gave me any list of bank accounts or anything like that."

"I surely did," Nan said crossly. "I think you've just forgotten."

"Well, it's possible," Doreen said. "If I did, I'm sorry.

It's not triggering, but then I have seen an awful lot of paperwork lately."

Nan chuckled. "That's exactly what you saw," she said. "I gave you that stack of paperwork to scan in for me. Remember?"

And, in fact, Doreen did remember. "That's right," she said. "I'd forgotten about that. But I didn't look at that stuff. It was yours."

"Foolish child," Nan said. "That had everything. The bank accounts, my lawyer, and I think the will was in there too."

"Maybe," she said, "but I don't remember."

"Well, you sent a digital copy to me, so you can take a look at what you have," she said, "because it's there somewhere."

"Maybe," she said. "I'll search for it."

"Do that then. Because you know something? If I happen to be the next little old gray-haired lady who drops dead, you'll have to deal with my estate."

And, on that note, Nan hung up, leaving Doreen staring in shock at her phone.

Chapter 10

Sunday Late Morning ...

DOREEN WALKED INSIDE her house, ignoring the temptation to return to the crime scene at Rosemoor, knowing they would be winding down now since the coroner had shown up. She knew Mack would arrive here soon anyway. A bit of coffee was left, but it was cold, so she put it in a large mug and put it in the fridge to drink later, if it ended up being a hot day. Then she put on a fresh pot. She was more disturbed than she wanted to be by Nan's parting words.

The fact that Nan had multiple safety deposit boxes, and one was full of all kinds of mysteries bothered her more than she had expected, but even worse was Nan's comment about being the next gray-haired lady to drop dead—although Nan had gone to dying her hair this lavender hue lately. But Doreen didn't know if that was in response to the ladies who were dropping dead. Even if Doreen thought some typecasting might be going on here, Nan wouldn't be that type.

But, for all the people who loved Nan, Doreen was sure some didn't love her. Just her gambling alone put her on the wrong side for a lot of people. Doreen loved Nan because of who she was to her, and Doreen didn't care about the rest, but not everybody looked at it that way. And wasn't that sad too because Nan was a very special person. It didn't change anything as far as who she was or wasn't, but the fact of the matter was, the thought of losing Nan was enough to depress Doreen thoroughly. She'd only just found her grandmother again, and Doreen didn't want to miss out on sharing any more time with her. It was still on her thoughts when a hard rattle came at her door.

Startled, she turned to look up as Mack stepped inside. He frowned at her. "What's the matter?" His voice was harsher than he expected as it immediately gentled, and he said, "Sorry, I didn't mean to startle you, but you look like you're upset."

She waved her phone at him. "It's Nan," she said. "Just that the last thing she said to me was that I needed to know about some safety deposit boxes and other stuff in case she ended up being the next little old lady who drops dead."

Mack's frown was instantaneous and broad. "I don't think she'd be the next one. There's no reason to think that."

"But the fact of the matter is," Doreen said, "you don't know. That's four little old ladies now. *Four.* Yes, one death isn't suspicious on its own, unless by other facts. But possibly two similar deaths could be connected. And three is a stretch to believe they aren't connected, not with all the female victims being roughly the same age and with the presence of the kiwis. But a fourth death, so much like the previous three, all in just a matter of days? No way are those four deaths not connected. That is an impossibility. They are connected. You know that."

"I do," he said. "And we'll put some security on Rosemoor, but that doesn't necessarily have anything to do with—"

"It's still pretty horrific to think about," she whispered.

He nodded gently. "It is. But I'm sure Nan has a lot of outspoken years left to survive," he said jokingly.

She smiled through the sudden wash of tears in her eyes. She brushed them away impatiently. "You know what? I woke up tired this morning, but that conversation with her just set me off on a downward spiral."

"Well then, let's grab coffee and sit out in the sun," he said.

"Do you have to go back to work?"

"No, not at the moment," he said. "It's technically my day off, and other people will be there."

"What about investigating the death?"

"Forensics is still on the scene. We've got one team doing the notification."

"I thought you would have done it," she said.

"Arnold knows Rosie," he said, "so he wanted to do it."

"Interesting," she said. "I guess everybody here knows Rosie. Everybody's related to everybody, aren't they?"

"To a certain extent, yes," he said. "But you know that it doesn't always work out quite that way."

"I see," she said. But she didn't really see anything. "So much for the deck, huh?"

"Well, originally," he said, "we weren't expecting it to be done this weekend anyway. We got a lot done yesterday." As he looked at her, he smiled. "It's all the stuff that you probably didn't realize would take so much time."

She nodded. "I really didn't."

"We're almost to the point of doing the decking boards," he said. He stepped down out the back, holding a cup of coffee carefully in his hand. "I can do a little bit more today, but I'll probably end up going back into the office and working on this case."

"This case is very important," she said immediately. "Outside of an inconvenience for me, the deck here isn't much of a problem."

Just then a shout came from the side of the house and in walked Wilbur.

Mack looked over and the two slapped hands.

"It's just you here today?" Wilbur asked.

"We got a DB this morning," Mack said.

"Ah," he said. "I wasn't on dispatch over the weekend, so I didn't hear about it. That's too bad. You guys could have had this done."

"Well, a few people could be showing up," Mack said. "But, if it's just me, I won't get anywhere today."

"Well, the two of us are here," he said. "I could probably call a couple of the guys and see if they can come in. It's just the decking boards now?"

"Steps," he said. "We were all set to start cutting stringers this morning."

"Right," he said. "Steps would be very important. You know what? A buddy of mine does stairs all the time. Let me give him a shout and see if he's got an hour. If we can get them cut and placed, I can start slinging in decking boards or at least that's a simple-enough job to do yourself."

"Right."

And then Wilbur turned to look around and asked, "Wasn't Tony supposed to come with his concrete mixer?"

"I was hoping so," Mack said, "but not everybody has time to spare."

"I hear you," he said. "Well, let me make a call." He walked toward his truck, talking on his phone. When he returned a few minutes later, he said, "Tony is on his way, and so is this buddy of mine, Warren. He's got a couple stencils that he uses for simple jobs with two steps. He said he'll bring those and a circular saw. We can get them cut and put in place, then it's literally laying decking boards."

"I know," Mack said. "And railings of course."

While Doreen sat here in the open doorway, her feet hanging over the open edge and staring at the wood that looked like it should be almost done but wasn't, of course, she smiled to hear other vehicles arriving. "Somebody's coming," she said, looking at Mack. As one man came around, and Wilbur introduced her to Warren. She smiled at Warren and said, "I think I know you. Don't I?"

He nodded. "I was one of the scuba divers who helped bring out that little boy, Paul," he said, shaking her hands. "And I'm more than happy to come and spend a few hours getting you a deck."

"Well, we certainly appreciated you doing the scuba diving," she said.

"Not a problem," he said. "I'm related to the family of the handyman who went into the river with Paul, and that was a mystery we wanted solved for a long time. A lot of totally undeserved hard feelings remained over that, so we were more than happy to see it resolved."

"Right. In that case, are you the stair guy?"

He chuckled. "I am, indeed, and I brought a couple stencils."

With that, they heard a couple shouts, and more men appeared, who had been here previously working on her house, plus a couple new guys came.

Mack looked at her and smiled. "You better make sure more cold beer is in the fridge."

"Can you stay?" she asked in a hurried whispered.

"Not for long," he said with a shrug. "But I can come back too."

She nodded and got up, then put on another pot of coffee and loaded the fridge with the last of the beer, hoping it was enough and realizing she would need to order more pizza. When she went back out, Mack was rousting up the work and setting up a quick and simple organizational strategy. She didn't know all the men, but she recognized quite a few of them. She talked with a couple as Mack disappeared, and the stairs started. Some of the men started framing up something, and she wasn't exactly sure what that was. She walked over to Tony and said, "I hate to be nosy, but what are you doing?"

He sat back on his haunches and grinned up at her. "Somebody said you wanted a patio."

She clapped her hands together. "I really want a patio," she said.

And he said, "You don't have anything alongside the house here, and it would be good to have it where you could also hose it off and sweep it." And he showed her how he was framing in a sidewalk from the front driveway all along the back and then to where the garden shed was. The sidewalk swerved into the patio area. Instead of a square patio, it was more of an oval, or at least it looked curved. She wasn't sure what it would end up being. And then a pathway went down to the creek.

She smiled. "I don't know how much you can do today, but this looks phenomenal."

"Well, I had quite an experience yesterday when I went to check out the concrete I had," Tony said, standing up. "I had about eight bags that I was willing to donate but needed more, so I went to the supply store to see what I could get for a deal. When I told the guy what I needed it for, and he gave me twenty bags free of charge."

She stared at him, and her jaw dropped. "Seriously? Why's that?"

"Because little Crystal," he said, "was this guy's student at school. And he worried and fretted and wondered for a long time. And he ended up quitting his teaching job and going into the family business, which was the big concrete business downtown, because he was so heartbroken over her. Now that you've solved that case, he was more than happy to donate concrete."

Doreen nodded, a little choked up at this display of appreciation for what she had done. She sniffled and wiped away the tears that had fallen. Tony kept on talking like she hadn't cried in front of him.

"And this is the easy-mix stuff, and I'm pretty sure, if we need more, we can go grab more."

"And how do we mix it?" she asked.

He pointed to a pickup backing up with this big rolling-looking thing in the back. "In this case," he said, "we'll do a lot of it by hand. So we'll space the two-by-fours as the break marks, and then we'll pour individual sections."

She was absolutely thrilled to realize that she was getting a patio at the same time. "If you give me the teacher's name," she said, "I'd be more than happy to call him and thank him. I'm so happy to see this come together."

Chapter II

Sunday Afternoon …

T ONY QUICKLY GAVE Doreen the name and the phone number of the teacher; then she stepped off to the side and called him. And when Ron Howard answered, and she explained who she was, he laughed and said, "I'm more than happy to do it, and those bags aren't anywhere near enough to repay you. Let me think about it. Maybe I'll send over a pallet, and you can just call us, and we'll bring back whatever you don't need." And she laughed in delight. When she returned to Tony, she told him what Ron had said.

Tony nodded, smiled, and said, "That's huge."

"Do we need to have all the deck done first?"

He shook his head. "No, as long as we know where the markers are and where the steps are," he said, "we'll block it off and take the concrete right up to the edge."

It was an even busier and more chaotic morning and afternoon compared to the day before, and she didn't think that was possible. Mack came. Mack left. Mack came again, and then Mack left again. When he came back the third time, it was three o'clock. He walked over, whispered to her, and said, "Offer the beer."

She gasped and cried out. "I forgot," she said. "So much is going on and everyone was so busy. I think that it's safe to walk up here on the deck now, isn't it?"

Mack went to talk to a couple guys and then held out his hand, helping her onto the first step, the second step, and then up to her new deck. The deck and stairs were solid and secured well. "Wow," she said, staring at the massive deck around her now. Stairs were on the front and on the side to get down around the house to the driveway. And a patio was happening. She was shocked. "This is really beautiful."

Just then Tony walked over and asked, "Did you want a garden along here? You don't have steps here. I know a railing is going up, but we wondered if you wanted something like a two-foot band here, where you could put something that climbs."

She nodded immediately. "Yes, please," she said. "I could put a trellis and the clematis or something up here. That would look gorgeous." So they cut into their sidewalk framing on the side and gave her a two-foot solid band for about six feet, and then they did the same on the other side. As she watched, they framed up boards to go all the way around the edge. She looked at Mack and said, "Can you believe I'm getting a deck and a patio?"

He chuckled. "I am not surprised." He walked into the kitchen. and she followed him. "Let's get the beer out," he said. "We don't want them to take too much of a break if things are really happening now."

She watched in surprise and realized that the concrete was already being poured. "Is this a big truckload or what? He said he would send over a pallet of bags."

Mack immediately halted at the sound of a big truck backing up with its *beeps* reverberating through the yard. He headed over and said, "What's this?"

Tony laughed. "I guess our concrete guy decided to screw that. We've got five yards here, which is lots for our purpose," he said, "and it's been tinted ever-so-slightly to a beautiful rustic color for the patio. We're desperately trying to finish off this framework so we can start pouring."

Doreen was close enough to hear him, and she asked, "Really, so no mixing?"

Tony shook his head. "This is the best-case scenario ever," he said. "He'll back up, and we've brought a couple wheelbarrows, plus we have yours, Doreen. So we'll move the wet concrete manually because we don't have a pumper truck to get it around the side of the house."

All those technical terms were driving her crazy, but she was quite happy to stand here with two six-packs in her hands as the men immediately started moving concrete. She looked over at Mack and held up the six-packs. He shrugged.

One of the guys working on the deck walked over and said, "I'll take one of those."

She smiled, snapped it off its plastic ring, and held it out to him.

He said, "If we can get the steps at least in place, then we won't have to step over the concrete."

"Oh my," she said. "I guess, all of a sudden, we're backing up against each other, aren't we?"

He laughed, took a heavy slug of his beer, and plunked it down on the deck, then jumped back over and started working again pretty quickly on the wooden steps. While Tony and some others worked on pouring the concrete sidewalk by the side of the house, Warren said, "I need to get this cut fast before the concrete pours." He looked at Doreen and added, "Because of the sawdust."

She gasped as the three of them immediately worked on the steps. The boards were cut, fitted, and nailed in place all the way from the front around the side and then stopped for the piece that would get a little bit of a railing and garden trellis on either side and then the shorter steps were put down on Richard's side of her house. And, all of a sudden, she watched as concrete started coming, wheelbarrow by wheelbarrow, all the way around to the far side of the house. And one guy was straightening and filling, making a sidewalk along the side too. "Too bad we can't have some all along this side of the house," she said.

"You probably can," Tony said. "We've still got all the bags yet that I came with. That's enough to do this too. But right now, we have to deal with the truck because that concrete has to keep churning, and we've only got a certain time period before it's no good anymore."

She stepped back immediately as the men ran wheelbarrow after wheelbarrow to the truck to fill up what was all the framed space in front of her here. Mack tucked her off to the side and said, "The dust is horrific, so let's just keep you back and out of the way."

"Are they supposed to do it by wheelbarrow?"

"If they have to, they will, yep," he said. "It's pretty normal, and it saves you a thousand-plus for a pumper truck."

"Well, I really could use the savings on the thousand dollars," she said, "because that would be a huge dig into my money."

"You might have gotten a deal down to $700," he said, "but, chances are, with them having to go and wash out the truck again, that would be another $150 fee too."

She rolled her eyes at him, confused. "This stuff is so

much money," she said. Three wheelbarrows ran back and forth. "Is there any way to see what they're doing?"

He led her alongside the fence to see better. A chute coming off the concrete truck delivered concrete, slowly filling up a wheelbarrow, and then it was stopped, and that wheelbarrow would disappear, and another one would load up. It would fill up, then stop, until the third one got in position. And, by the time the third one was done, the first one was back. And the men were literally running. This kept on going for almost an hour. And then the truck driver said, "This should be almost it."

"Looks good," Tony said. "We're still short a little bit, but if you've got a couple more wheelbarrow loads in there …"

"We'll see," the trucker said. "You've got whatever I've got here. It's a hefty five yards, but I'm not sure that's quite enough."

"We've got some concrete we can mix too, for that matter, but I don't have the same tint," Tony said. "As long as everything along that one side is the same. Looks like we've still got a bunch here, so do all the back on the far side and then see if we can get this sidewalk here run. After that, we can do my concrete bags over on the far side, and that won't be too bad. We still must move the materials off that side so that we can frame up the sidewalk though."

And, sure enough, by the time they were done, one wheelbarrow full sat there, waiting for somebody to determine where it needed to go. She was amazed at the amount of concrete that had just been leveled onto her place, and, as she watched, men were straightening and doing some weird up-and-down pounding in it and then smoothing it out. Mack tried to explain the different stages, and she was seriously fascinated. The sidewalk went right up to the front of the house, and she was amazed. But that meant there was absolutely no way for anybody to walk on either side of her house, except for about a six-inch space alongside the fence. They'd paved a walkway, a patio, and a path down to the creek.

"I guess now, gravel along the edge there?"

"Gravel and maybe some spray to stop any weeds coming through," Tony said. "And you'll need to put a little bit alongside the house there too because we can't pour concrete right up against it."

She nodded. "And that'll probably be a truckload of gravel too."

"No," he said. "A couple yards. Not very much land here. And, on the other side, you have to do the same."

It didn't take much more than another thirty minutes to an hour, and, all of a sudden, the concrete was done. As she looked, all the stairs had boards and so did all the top of the deck. And suddenly it all came to an end. She stared at it in shock, at her beautiful deck, and noted that two of the men were putting in railings, one to go down the steps on the side and one to go along the top of the deck down one side. They had several support posts in place.

She smiled. "That's like perfect timing."

"It is." Mack stood beside her.

As she watched, the men popped a railing piece between two supports and screwed it in then repeated it until the one side was done.

"Wow," she said as the process was repeated on the steps down again to the side of the house, where the second railing was put in, anchoring one end of it to the wall of the house as well. And then, she looked at the big front expanse of her deck, facing the creek, and asked, "Do we need a railing there?"

Mack shook his head. "No, it looks perfect."

And, with that, all the men stepped back, a beer in their hand, to take a look at the job well done.

"That looks absolutely phenomenal," she said warmly. "I can't believe it."

"Well, we need to put a sealer coat on all the wood," one of the men said, who'd just popped the railing on. "And it looks like it'll rain tomorrow, so we should probably push to get that done."

"Well, I got my concrete mixer here," Tony said. "We'll pour the rest of the walkway on the far side of the house, and then all the concrete work is done too."

She watched one of them gently brooming in a beautiful little pattern into the concrete, and it went all the way down the side of the house and to the patio. She looked back down to the creek.

Mack nodded. "Depends on whether you're still getting some more concrete or not," he said, "but we can manually pour blocks all the way down."

"I've got one of those flagstone block templates," one of the guys said. "It's at home. I think I have four of them." With the guys bugging him, he said, "Okay. Hey, I don't mind if we'll do another couple hours. I'll need food, but I can run home and grab that."

"Oh, my goodness," Doreen said. "I'm happy to order more pizza."

"Pizza it is," the guy said, cheering. "Make sure there's more beer too."

She laughed and said, "I'll check that."

And, with Mack at her side, she headed up to the kitchen. Two more six-packs were still in the fridge. She looked at it and frowned. "Is that enough?" she asked.

He shook his head. "Another six-pack would be better."

"I don't even know how to get that," she said.

"Right," he said. "It's a matter of figuring out what everybody'll want."

"I don't have pop either."

"No," he said, "but you can order that to be delivered with the pizza." He called out to the guys outside. "Anybody want some pop with pizza?"

"Absolutely," a quorum of voices raised up, answering him.

So they quickly put together another pizza and pop order, and she called it in. When they said it would be ready in about an hour, she nodded and said, "Thank you." Then she walked back outside and said, "Okay, sixty minutes to pizza, and we've got pop coming too. I'm putting on coffee, and there's still some beer."

"You got it all," one of the guys said, smiling at her.

"What I've got," she said in all seriousness, "is the best darn group of men I never even thought I had. You have no idea how much this means to me."

"Hey," one of them said, "we're happy to help. You've done a lot for this community too." The others nodded in agreement.

"Well, I wasn't thinking about that," she said. "I mean, I try to solve some of these problems so that it brings closure for the families. You don't really think about the extras in life when you do that."

"Because you don't think of it," one of them said, "it can happen easily."

She nodded and smiled. "So, now what are we doing

with the bags of cement?" She watched as a couple of the men wheeled over another big round barrel thing.

"We'll toss it in here, and we'll mix in some sand," Tony said. "I've got a bunch of that in my truck, and we'll add in some gravel. That ends up as concrete. Then we'll pour enough to put a path down on the far side of the house. In order to do that, we'll frame it up, put down a gravel bed, like we did for the patio and the walkway, and then pour down the concrete. We can do it nice, but it won't be the same look. It'll be more cobblestony."

"I'm happy with cobblestones," she said. "And, besides, the pattern on the first sidewalk is fairly cobblestony."

"And I actually only did that," one of the guys said, and she thought his name was Harry, "when I realized one of the other guys had cobblestone molds for the path. So now it'll match a little at least."

Chapter 12

Sunday Late Afternoon …

BY THE TIME the pizzas arrived, the guy had returned with his templates. And she cried out in amazement when she saw the heavy-duty plastic forms. He had five of them, which he laid down in a row—from her patio to the creek—and then they just filled them with concrete. So, as they were working on filling the forms and then having to wait for them to dry enough that they could take them off and reuse them, the guys did some other work. They poured a big flat piece alongside the house.

Because they had to hand mix it, and it wouldn't be done as one big pour, like earlier with the big truck, each batch of concrete could be mixed and poured separately. It would leave a crack—like how bathroom tiles needed grout in between—but that was totally okay too. They'd fill in with dirt or rock. Immediately her mind thought of a moss she could walk on for those spaces.

It wouldn't match the other side, but how many people actually walk this far side of the house? It would stop the weeds completely though, and they put it up almost against the side of the house. Gravel would again be needed for that final bit. As she watched that whole side of her house transform, it took about an hour. And when the men were done with that, she arrived with a big pizza deluxe with everything on it and opened it up right there for them.

The men grinned and grabbed. "That wasn't hard at all," Tony said. "It looks good."

One of the men said. "I've got some dye with me, but it won't be an exact match. Still should be close enough as the two colors won't be butted up against each other. I've been working on it over here." And he showed her what he'd been experimenting with on a piece of board with some of the leftover concrete. And it was a darn close match. Mostly a brown look but it was nice.

She smiled. "You know what? I think that'll look really nice."

"Good," he said. "Because, after we eat, we'll start mixing and pouring more blocks to make a small walkway and edge along the gardens, one on the right, one on the left."

"How long does it take to dry?"

The guy tinting the concrete looked to Tony to answer.

"It's hard to say," Tony said. "Depends on the weather. Concrete can take seventy-two hours to cure. If it rains, it would be perfect. Still we'll soak it down several times anyway."

She looked at him in astonishment.

Tony smiled. "Water helps concrete cure," he explained. "And it helps it to set, so it's a good thing if it does rain. That's why we're pushing it right now because it's calling for rain. Now I don't want it to rain until the concrete is down." Tony stared up at the growing cloudy sky and nodded. "Have you guys got one more hour together? That's probably what we'll need."

"What about the forms though?" she asked, motioning at them.

He nodded. "I have more in the truck. But that is a bit of a concern. It depends. We didn't pour them very thick, so what we really need to do is leave the forms on as long as we can. I do have quite a few, so we'll see how it goes." They did over twenty forms before they sat back and took a look.

Just then Tony's phone rang. He laughed as he talked to someone, and, even as he spoke, he walked to the front, returning with another man, carrying more forms.

She smiled at that. They mixed up more concrete and filled more forms. By now everyone was working fast, as they were up against the weather. She overheard them discussing when to remove the templates. "Is it safe to do that so soon? Will the concrete blocks lose their shape?"

"Well," Tony said, "they could slip a little bit along the edges if you walk on it too early, but, other than that, I don't think it'll be a problem." He looked over at his buddy. "What do you think?"

"No, I don't think so. We added some stuff to help it firm up nicely," he said. "I didn't leave mine for very long. Who's got time? I suggest we do another five and get some more food and see how it's doing." Each one of the forms was about four feet long, so she already had a good sixty feet of stonework done now on the one side and forty already on the other. If they could give her another twenty feet before it rained ...

"The thing is," Tony said as they finished up, "no weight is allowed on this at all for at least two days. I'd prefer to leave the forms longer, but ... at least it's got the additives for quick forming."

She nodded. She'd kept all her animals inside because so

many more people were out here, and, without the usual steps off the kitchen's back door, it was a problem. She had the screen door open, so that the animals could see her, but her pets had not seemed too bothered. She also realized how stuck they were, with no backyard access. She couldn't go around the left or the right. "I guess there's no way to get out here for the next couple days, is there?"

Tony shook his head. "No, gotta let all the concrete cure. I'll come back tomorrow and grab my mixer," he said. "That's okay by me, if it's not a problem for you."

"No," she said. "I'm totally okay with that."

And it wasn't long before the next five forms were done. Now she had about twenty feet more on this side, making a total of sixty feet down both sides. Tony looked back toward the creek and started measuring off. "We'll need a bit more," he said. "Let's take a break, eat, and see. In the worst-case scenario, I have to return tomorrow to mix the rest."

As she looked around, the men were already pouring some finishing product all over the wood on the deck. She looked at Mack. He had a paintbrush in his hand and a slice of pizza in the other. He was busy putting a stain on the railing and the handle and the top post. "Wow," she said, walking up to him. "That looks phenomenal."

He nodded. "It sure does."

She stood nearby, staring in awe, especially with the fresh and shiny look all over it. "Will that be dry in time before the rain?"

"It's pretty quick-drying stuff," he said. "And it's soaking into the wood. It's fast dry for about 75 percent of each coat, and the rest will take another day or so to cure."

"Perfect," she said.

He looked at her, smiled, and said, "Then you do another coat."

Her face fell. "Oh," she said. "That'll be a little harder."

"Not only that," he said, "but you also have to sand it all."

"Oh my," she said. "Really?"

"Yes, if you want to do it properly. A lot of people skip that step, but it's important if you want the wood smooth."

"Interesting," she said. "That'll take quite a while."

"Yeah, and you'll need a little sander," he said. "And I might be able to lend you one."

She smiled. "You know what? I might just have one."

"You just might," Mack said. "I'll look. You don't want to be doing this by hand."

"No," she said with a groan. "I definitely don't."

As it was, she was full up on pizza. She'd had some of the pop herself too and felt like the whole world was a different place right now. Not only did she have a gorgeous deck but she had a huge patio, and she had both sides of the house taken care of with proper concrete walkways, so she didn't have to worry about weeds on the sides of her home, and had this gorgeous stone walkway down the middle of the yard from the patio to the creek.

And now she had these narrow cobblestone pathways going all the way around the garden too. She looked along the side and wondered if she should take the edger and cut back the grass or let it grow alongside the walkway. She walked back to where Tony was removing five forms from the initial steps poured and was setting up another five forms to fill. "Are they drying that fast?"

He shook his head. "Not really," he said, "but they're keeping their edge. The inside is pretty jiggly, even with something extra to help it set faster. So we're adding a frame to keep them contained." He pointed back to where his buddy had installed a simple two-by-four framework all along the edges.

"Oh, that's a good idea," she said as she smiled. "Should I cut the lawn back along here, so I can keep mowing it, or maybe put gravel in here too, or do I let the grass grow right up to the concrete?"

"It would probably do really fine with crushed rocks through here," he said. "That way, you won't have to worry about the weeds coming through, and you'll have a clean, crisp line that you can run the lawn mower tires on."

She liked that idea. And it gave her something that she could do. She grabbed her edger and started cutting back a nice, neat trim line. "I'll have to get some gravel in," she said.

"I can leave you what I've got leftover here," he said. "We already took some and filled in the gap between the house and the sidewalk, then also the gap in between the fence and the sidewalk. We'll do the same along the far side of the house and that newest sidewalk, but you probably want to fill in this section too."

"What about landscape cloth? Is that an issue if I don't lay that down first?"

"I wouldn't think so," he said. "But if you give it quite a bit of rock in here, the weeds won't be much of a problem."

She nodded, wondering about that because she did have some landscape cloth. But then it seemed like it was more trouble than it was worth half the time. By the time she had edged down to the creek, she could see that they had chosen to put the complete two-by-four frame all the way along each walkway. Although she thought she had a lot of spare wood at this point, there wasn't any now. As a matter of fact, it looked like they were coming up a little bit short as it was.

She walked back to the house to inspect her supply stash, but they had moved it all to pour that first sidewalk. So the leftover wood was in the backyard, half in her garden and half out. She lifted a couple boards and took a serious look, but it seemed like nothing was left. They'd used up almost everything. Two boards were left, and they looked like decking boards. Then she spied a couple pieces of two-by-fours and a couple pieces of the huge six-by-sixes or eight-by-eights that had been used under the deck.

Not much was left. All the bags of cement would be used up shortly per Tony, and all the anchors had been used, and she guessed all the screws had gone into securing the deck boards. She hadn't had to buy anything, except for those screws and the beer and the pizza this weekend. She smiled at that because, if there was ever cheap labor, this buddy system had to be the best kept secret in the world.

As she walked back down to the creek, Tony poured the fifth of the last group of steps along the garden edge. The first ones were still holding with space in between, although a little bit of it was shifting. "It looks phenomenal," she said in wonder.

"It really is," he said. "That additive helped it to set really fast, and so, like I said, we're hoping that it'll keep its shape with the two-by-fours."

"I'm grateful to have it even like this," she said.

"It looks really cool, doesn't it?" he said happily. "We're at about sixty feet here, and you'll need at least one or two more."

"I can see that," she said, "but probably not full forms though, right?"

"I don't think so." He looked at the cut grass and nodded. "I can't get around here with the rest of the gravel," he said. "We did only what we could reach from the front, so the rest of this'll wait until tomorrow."

"It's probably better anyway," she said, "because you've got to take the boards off the main path too."

"In that case, we should leave the gravel for the day after," he said. "I can pretty well dump the rest of it up in your driveway, and we can move it around in the wheelbarrow, once the concrete cures fully."

"Hey, so much has been done already," she said. "I just can't believe it."

"It's almost a complete transformation back here," he said. "You've obviously put a lot of work into the gardens too."

"I'm getting there," she said. "I did pick up a bunch of plants from Heidi recently." Remembering that brought up a frown on her face.

"Is that the woman you put into jail?" He laughed. "It doesn't sound like people really appreciate you too much, do they?"

"No," she said. "I keep trying to make friends, but I end up putting them in jail instead."

At that, he burst out a big guffaw.

"I wanted to have some of the extra plants that she didn't want," she said.

"My mom's got a ton," he said. "I'll talk to her about it and maybe let her know that you're looking for some."

"Sure," she said. "I'd appreciate that."

"Doreen," Mack called.

She looked over to see him waving at her, and she headed that way. "Hey," she said. "What's up?"

"A bunch of guys are leaving," he said. "Can't do anything more with the wood now as the first stain coat is done.

You've only got about a quarter of this can left. That might be enough for a second coat because the first coat sucked up into the wood pretty good, but it's hard to tell."

"So we might have to get more?"

He nodded. "And we'll keep all these rollers and stuff for Monday," he said. "And, like I said, we'll still sand everything before we do a second coat."

"Is the second coat enough?"

He nodded. "It should be. You could have left it without that because these are treated decking boards, but this will extend their life."

She smiled. "I'm totally okay to do whatever's needed," she said.

"That's what I figured," he said.

She walked over to the men who were leaving, shook their hands, and said, "Thank you so very much."

"Not a problem," one said. And about six of them took off.

"Wow," she said to Mack. "I don't even know who all of them were."

He leaned over and whispered, "Not sure I do either." She laughed, then turned to face her newly redone backyard. Tony worked down at the far end by the creek, and she walked down with Mack to see him.

"This is lovely," Mack said, raising a hand to his forehead. "That pathway along the garden edge really sets off the whole yard."

"I'm really happy," she beamed.

Tony nodded. "It looks great. We've done a ton today."

"Yeah, we did," Mack said. "I can't believe it's all happened."

"Exactly."

As Mack and Doreen headed toward the house, people still milled around.

"What are we doing next?" one of the guys asked.

"Not a whole lot," Mack said. "It's just clean up now. Also, if you think about it, it's quite late."

She looked at him and asked, "Is it?"

"Yeah. It's 7:30 already."

"Wow," she said. "I can't believe it." And, indeed, the day had gone so fast. "Did you learn anything about Rosie yet?"

"No," he said. "The guys have been covering for me, so I could be here for a lot of this, but I will go back now."

"Did you get any pizza?"

"I did," he said. "But I'll have more before I leave." And very quickly, there was just her and Tony and the two guys working with him. She brought down a couple more beers for them and asked if they wanted some pizza. They all agreed to have more of both.

Chapter 13

Sunday Early Evening ...

DOREEN GRABBED ANOTHER box of pizza, walked through the front door and gingerly made her way to the backyard, and said, "This is all leftover, so eat up." The men grinned and kept digging. She left it on a nearby chair for them and watched as more concrete was mixed, and then she looked at Tony. "Do we have enough concrete?"

"Actually," he said, "we're coming to the end of it. So, what I'm hoping for is that the last bag finishes off the rest of it for you."

"Now that would be very nice," she said.

And, indeed, as she watched, one of the men said, "Those were the last bags right there. And they're empty as it's all in the mixer right now."

They had just finished pouring the last of the concrete pathway to the edge of her property. She smiled. "I never thought," she said, "not in a million years, that we'd get all this done. I couldn't have even hoped for all the concrete work. It looks stunning."

"Especially the way it started, huh?"

"Well, it was a pretty rough beginning," she said. One of

the men who had been working with the concrete was a cop named Bruce, she thought. She asked him, "Were you involved in that last body found near the creek, the fourth old woman to die?"

Bruce nodded. "It makes me want to go check on my grandma."

"Right?" she said with a nod. "I feel the same way about my nan."

"I don't think it's contagious," Mack said, "but it's definitely suspicious."

"Well, a couple drugs can mimic heart attacks," one guy said. She looked at him in surprise. He shrugged and said, "My dad is a doctor."

She beamed at him. "Perfect," she said. "But watch it. I might have some questions for you some time."

He laughed and laughed. "Hey, I've been following your antics with great interest," he said. "My wife is a huge fan."

She smiled and asked, "So, which drugs cause heart attacks?"

He smiled back and said, "Well, it depends." And he reamed off several drugs that could cause accidental deaths, like drug overdoses can do too, and other drugs that could induce what looked like a heart attack event. Then he added, "Honestly, if they're on IVs at all during the night, it's pretty easy to add to that setup. You know that digitalis and blood thinners could do it too." He gave a couple other chemical names that she didn't know.

She pulled out her phone, hit Record, and said, "Would you say those again?" He quickly repeated them so she could do some research on that later. She looked at Mack. "I guess the coroner will test for these, won't they?"

He nodded. "Absolutely, he will."

"Good," she said, "but we also need to look into that lovely grandson."

"Need a motive," he said.

"There'll be a motive," she said. "But it's hard to place the other deaths on him though."

"Unless they were test runs," the doc's son said. "A couple cases not too long ago involved people trying out different methods to see what worked the best in order to kill the one person they wanted to kill."

She stared at him and shook her head. "Wow, that sounds so typical of some people, doesn't it?"

He nodded. "Some of them are not the easiest people in the world to understand."

"That's one way to look at it," she said.

He grinned at her and said, "My wife wanted me to take a picture of your animals, but you've kept them inside." As he looked around at all the wet concrete, he nodded and said, "Then considering all this, that's exactly where they should be."

She laughed. "As you leave today," she said, "I'll take you inside, and you can meet the gang."

"Well, that would give me an excuse for being late tonight," he said, beaming. "The only reason I got to come was because it was your house."

"Sounds like you and your wife have a lovely marriage," she said, chuckling.

"He's under lock and key," Tony said with a big and affable grin. "And that's the way he likes it."

She smiled. "Hey, if you can make a marriage work for you, all the power to you."

The men had many jokes regarding marriage right now, and, as she listened to them, she realized that some were married and some weren't. Tony was divorced and living with a second girlfriend. And another guy, whose name was Sam, had been divorced four times. She looked at him in surprise.

He shrugged, smiled sheepishly, and said, "I keep falling in love."

"But do you fall out of love just as fast?" she asked cautiously.

The other men laughed. "I didn't think so," he said. "But apparently, I'm not there for the long term."

"What about your wives?"

"They aren't either somehow," he said. "But I really love the whole engagement stage, the first flush of marriage. After that, well, it's not quite the same anymore."

She chuckled. "So, how many are you going for? A half dozen?"

The others joked, "An even dozen."

"A baker's dozen," Mack said, chuckling.

Sam smiled and said, "I'll find true love one day." He looked over at Doreen. "Are you married?"

"Still working on the divorce," she said wistfully.

"But only one divorce?"

She laughed. "Personally I think one is enough for anyone," she said. "I don't want to go through it as many times as you."

"True enough," he said. But almost wistfully, he added, "But falling in love is beautiful."

She smiled at him. "Yes, I can see that," she said. "But then there's the rest of it."

And, for all that was said and done, it was suddenly time for everybody to pack up and go.

Chapter 14

Sunday Evening ...

WITH MACK AND everybody else gone, Doreen was exhausted. She struggled to get back inside her house, having to go around to the front door. All the tools and everything had been left as is because it was impossible to walk anywhere just yet. Boards were resting on top of the curing concrete framework though, little crossing bridges to make it easier to get around. And no one was allowed on the curing deck either, so everybody had to stay on the boards to get to the front yard. All promised to come back the next day to clean up. She smiled and said to Mugs, "I don't care honestly. It'll be gone tomorrow for sure. And I'll like being alone after all this togetherness."

He woofed, exhausted and unhappy that he'd been locked up inside all day but delighted that she was with him. "Let's go for a bit of a walk," she said, and she headed out the front door. She wanted to go down to the creek, but that would be a longer walk. So she headed toward Nan's instead. She pulled out her phone as she got closer and called Nan.

"Hello, Doreen," Nan answered, but her voice sounded tired and frail.

"I'm walking toward you," she said, "but I know it's late."

"It'd still be nice to see you," Nan said.

And just enough sadness was in the tone of her voice that Doreen picked up the pace. "We're right around the corner," she said.

"It's too late for tea," Nan said.

As Doreen got there, she could see Nan in a long fluffy housecoat. Feeling bad for having disturbed her, Doreen walked up to the patio and bent over to give her a big kiss. "Are you having an early night?"

"Yes," Nan said. "I admit that Rosie's death hit me a little harder than I ever expected."

"I'm so sorry," Doreen said. "I know it's tough to lose a friend at any time. But when you think something wrong is going on …"

"Well, I can't help but think that that grandson might have done something to move her along."

"It's possible," she said.

"I don't want to even think about any more of my friends passing."

"It's hard to be left behind, isn't it?" Doreen whispered gently.

Nan's eyes filled with tears. "That's the thing," she said. "It's really tough to watch everybody go before you. It's hard to be the one left behind, yet I don't want to leave you behind."

"And I appreciate that," Doreen said. "I'll never be ready to lose you."

Nan patted her hand, and they sat here, comfortable and enjoying the evening air. Doreen didn't want to stay too long though, so she said, "Please don't go for any walks on your own."

"No," Nan said. "Not until you solve this." She smiled up at her. "I know you'll do Rosie justice."

"Nan, I know you believe in me," Doreen said, "but you can't put too much on me with this one because it is an active investigation."

"I know," she said. "But, by the time the drug test results come back to prove that she was given something, it'd be awfully hard to have waited that long."

"That's true," Doreen said. "Who is this grandson any-way?"

"He's been in her room all day," Nan said with a sniff. "Trying to clean it out, but I don't know what's there to clean out."

"Is he here now?" she asked.

"I'm not sure. Maybe," she said, looking back toward her apartment. "I'm pretty tired of having anything to do with him. He's just so despicable."

"Is that really true though, that he wanted her to die early?" Doreen asked.

"I don't know," she said. "I know that Rosie was always worried about it. She was always afraid of him."

"And that's not nice," she said.

Just then they heard yelling inside.

Chapter 15

Sunday Evening ...

NAN IMMEDIATELY HOPPED to her feet, heading inside her apartment for her front door.

And, with Mugs racing beside her, Doreen followed Nan. "Do you know what this is about?"

"I'm not sure," she said. "I don't know who all that could be."

They went out to the hallway to find Richie berating a young man. Doreen reached over and gently patted Richie on the shoulder. "I understand everybody is upset," she said. "Let's just calm down now."

The young man looked at her, sneered, checking her from head to toe and back up again. "And who are you?"

Richie bristled, and Nan immediately got irate. Then the kid took a look at the animals at Doreen's feet, and his lip curled. "Oh, that's disgusting," he said. "A dog and a cat. What the hell's that on your shoulder? Some sort of a tumor?"

"Now I know who you are," Doreen said with a smile. "You must be the very greedy and ill-mannered grandson of poor Rosie. The fact of the matter is, the woman's not even cold yet, and here you are, trying to get your hands on her stuff."

"It's not like she's got anything anyway," he snapped.

"And why is that?" He sneered again. "It's not fair. There should be something for me."

"Why is that?" Doreen asked. "Why do you think you deserve anything?"

"She's got nobody else to leave it to," he said.

"I think a lot of cat shelters need donations," Doreen said, not liking this guy one bit. "And definitely some dog shelters need money too. I'm sure there is even one for birds somewhere, and Rosie would definitely like to help the animals."

Richie nodded. "She definitely would have," he said. "Why should you get any of her money?"

"Because I'm the only family she has, old man," Danny said, shoving his face into Richie's.

Immediately Doreen got into his face. "Elder abuse is not allowed in this place," she snapped. "Now you march yourself out of here, or else I'm calling the police."

"The police won't listen to you. You're nothing but a washed-up, drippy old maid," he said with that sneer once more. "Besides, this is my grandmother's place."

"Good. I'm glad you mentioned that," Doreen said. "Because it's the end of the month, and her rent is due. So you better fork out that money right now, young man. Otherwise, you've got no business coming here at all." She glared at him, but she had her phone out and was already dialing Mack.

"Who are you calling?" Danny asked. "Give me that phone." And he tried to grab the phone out of her hand.

Immediately Mugs started to growl. In a very soft voice,

Doreen told Danny, "Touch me again, and that dog will take your foot off."

He glared at her and down at Mugs. "You're some freaky lady," he said. "Nobody will listen to you."

"Well, we'll see," she said. "Because Richie's grandson is a cop too, and nobody touches my nan without Mack knowing about it."

Mack picked up the call and said, "Doreen, what's the matter?"

"Rosie's grandson is causing a stir and attacked poor Richie in Rosemoor, when he tried to stop him from messing up Rosie's room," she said. "I came down to visit Nan, and Danny's in the hallway, causing all kinds of commotion."

"He has no right to be in Rosie's room at all," Mack said, his voice harsh. "Who let him in?"

"I doubt anybody let him in. He's the scuttling little fish that would sneak his way into the place and search her room, not giving a darn about his own grandmother. But it's a crime scene now, isn't it?" she asked with a note of satisfaction. "So I suggest you get here right now and secure the room and make sure this guy spends the night in the jail."

"I'm not sticking around to be put in jail," Danny yelled. "What? Are you some weirdo? That's my grandmother's room."

"That does not make it *your* room," Doreen said. "And, in case you hadn't gotten the memo, her death wasn't normal, and they're treating this room as a crime scene. That means you've been interfering in her room, so you're not going anywhere."

"You can't stop me," he said. Then he shoved his face at her phone and said, "Neither can you, asshole." And he tried to turn and bolt.

But Mugs jumped up on his kneecap as he pivoted, and he tripped. As he went down, Goliath came out of nowhere and skidded along his back, leaving deep gouges in his shirt.

Danny screamed about being under attack.

"Doreen, what's the matter?" Mack cried out.

"Well, Danny made a threatening move on me, so Mugs and Goliath got a little defensive," she said. "Now Danny's on the ground, crying like a baby. Are you coming?"

"Do I have a choice?" he asked with a heavy sigh. "Darren is coming too. We'll be there in five."

She patted Richie, who was looking a little worse for wear after the confrontation. "Are you okay?"

He nodded. "I'd be fine except that Danny's still here."

Doreen looked at Danny on the floor and said, "You're such a loser."

"I'm not," he said, shifting to his knees.

"You tormented your poor grandmother for whatever few pennies she had," she snapped. "Whatever happened to you getting a job and looking after yourself?"

"I had a job," he said. "It's not my fault I got laid off."

"So what are you doing here, if it isn't searching her place for money?"

"I was looking for her will," he said. "It's supposed to be all mine."

"What's all yours?" she asked. "You said Rosie doesn't have anything."

"But something was paying for this room," he said. "This is not a cheap place to live in."

"No, it's not," she said, "but let's get real. Probably her pension was paying for this."

"It was her investments and savings," he snapped. "And they now come to me."

"Only if a will says so," she said. "But I wouldn't trust that anyway."

"Who is her lawyer?" Nan asked Danny.

"I don't know if she has a lawyer," Danny said, slowly getting to his feet and wiping the dirt off his clothes. He looked down at the dog and said, "If I ever see that dog come close to me again, I'll kick it."

"Well, that dog wouldn't have attacked you," a man said, his hard voice coming from down the hallway, "if you hadn't gone after Doreen."

The kid immediately turned and looked up at Mack, then frowned. "Hey, who are you?"

"I'm the cop she called on the phone," he said, crossing his arms.

Young Darren was here too. He walked immediately over to Richie. "Granddad, you okay?"

"You need to deal with him," Richie said, flicking a hand at Danny. "He was in poor Rosie's room, looking for anything he could steal."

Darren looked at Danny and frowned. "You have no rights to anything in that room," he said.

"She was my grandmother," Danny said. "I get anything of hers now."

"Good. Including her debts, I hope," Doreen said.

"No," he said. "Not her debts. I get her assets."

"Well, that isn't for you to choose on your own," Mack said. "Maybe a will gives you those rights."

"Well, there will be a will," he said, sticking his chin out pugnaciously. "We just have to find it. I was looking for it."

"I don't care if you were looking to find it or not," Mack said. "You've got no business being here."

"Well, you can't stop me," he said. "You aren't anybody

in power here."

"Not here at Rosemoor per se, but I'm the law," he said, "and I'm not giving you a choice. You'll go home now, and one of our lovely officers will take you there, so we can find out exactly where you live, and then we'll contact whatever lawyer was looking after Rosie's will, and we'll see whether you've been left anything or not."

Frustrated and obviously angry and upset at the turn of events, he turned, looked at Doreen, and glared at her. "I'll get you for this."

"Duly noted that you've now threatened me publicly in front of two officers of the law," she said in a calm voice.

Danny clenched his fists and took a step forward. Immediately Mugs growled. Danny looked down at Mugs and drew his leg back.

"I wouldn't do that if I were you," Nan said, her voice very deep. She stood stiff-backed, glaring at the young man. "Only the lowest of the low would attack an animal, particularly in anger."

At that, Mack grabbed Danny by the upper arm, then tugged him down the hallway.

"I think a night in jail would help him," Doreen said hopefully.

"No," Danny yelled. "That's not what'll happen."

"He did attack me," Doreen said. "What if I want to press charges, Mack?"

He turned, looked at her, and asked, "Do you?"

"How about we throw him in jail overnight, and I call it off tomorrow?"

He sighed. "And how about we send him home, and maybe, if he owes money to somebody else, they can find him instead."

"Hey, you can't do that," said the skinny kid.

"Why not?" Mack said, now pushing the kid who didn't want to be at the home.

"Because I do owe money to somebody," he said, and a note of desperation had entered his voice. "If they find me, I'm in trouble."

"And why is that our problem?" Doreen asked. "Here you were breaking into a woman's room who had just died to see what you could steal. Did you get her candy too?"

He turned and glared at her. "It's my candy now," he said with that sneer of his.

"Just because you are a living relative of Rosie's," she said, "doesn't mean you get everything."

For a moment, he stared at her. "Yes, it does."

Mack shook his head. "No, it doesn't. It depends on the will."

"Well, I was trying to get the will," he said, "but she and Richie wouldn't let me."

"Good thing," Darren said. "We don't want you upsetting the seniors here."

"Too late," Richie said, shaking a fist in Danny's direction. "I think the punk should be let go, so he can go back home again, and we'll see if the guys who he owes money to then find him."

And still screaming and squawking, Mack led the kid out of the old folks' home.

Doreen turned to look down at Nan. "Will you be able to sleep tonight?"

Nan let out a deep breath. "I'll have to calm down first," she said. She looked up at Richie. "I don't know. It's been a pretty rough day, hasn't it?"

"Absolutely," Richie said. "These young ones, they get

worse every time."

Nan nodded. She patted Doreen's hand. "Thank you so much for coming to our rescue," she said nodding at Rosie's room in front of her. "I'll miss her."

Doreen shook her head. "It breaks my heart to know that her sorry grandson's trying to take what little Rosie had," she said. The door was open to Rosie's room. "She was bringing me that note too, and I wish she had made it to my place, so I could have talked to her, could have seen what it was that she wanted me to do."

Richie asked her about the note, and she told him a condensed version. He sighed, then said, "She was really bothered about her grandson. She had talked to her lawyer about the will, but I don't know if she ever did anything to follow up on it."

"It's a tough situation," she said.

"I guess we wait and see whatever is in her room," Richie said.

Doreen turned to look at Darren and asked him, "Did you guys go through her room today?"

"Two officers did," he said. "I'm not sure if they found anything."

She hesitated. "And no way I'll be allowed to go in there and take a look, will I?"

Darren shook his head. "Can't let you do that."

"That's fine," she said, "but my name is on the Post-it Note on the wall up there. Can you at least go see what that says?"

He looked at her in surprise, then looked at the note on the wall and stepped into the room, while everybody crowded at the open doorway. "Remember to talk to Doreen." He looked back at her and said, "That would be the note you are talking about."

"Turn it over," she said. "You never know. Something might be on the back."

He lifted a corner of the note and nodded. "There is something." He removed the pushpin and flipped it over, then whistled.

"What's it say?"

"Must tell Doreen about the murders. She's the only one who will understand."

There was silence at first, and then everybody looked at each other before staring at Doreen. Her eyebrows shot up as she asked Darren, "Is there anything else?"

He shook his head slowly. "What do you know about any murders?" he asked, looking at Doreen suspiciously.

"Nothing," she said. "I know that she wanted to talk to me about something, so I was trying to see if she had left any notes about it herself here."

"No," he said. "Not at least at this point, at this place."

"Somebody needs to go in there and take another look," Nan said. "Why won't you let Doreen?"

Darren looked a bit haggard, as everybody pounded him with questions. Finally he put his hand up and said, "Stop. I'll ask Mack. Then it's on his head whether he lets Doreen in here or not." And he pulled out his phone and called Mack turning slightly away so no one was listening in. Not that anyone could hear Mack's side of the conversation.

Finally he put away his phone and said, "Doreen and only Doreen can come in. It's only because we've already had officers through here once." He crooked a finger and turned to Doreen. "You can come in."

She nodded and walked to the first light switch, then flipped it on. "Now let's take a look," she said with a big smile. And she headed straight to the night table.

"Why are you looking in there?" Darren asked.

"Because everybody knows that, when you have a small room, you put the important stuff—that you really want—closest to you at all times. Rosie spent most of her time in bed," she said, "so anything she wanted to keep close would be here in her night table." Doreen pulled out the drawer, dumped it on the bed, and then flipped it over. And, sure enough, taped underneath was an envelope with Doreen's name on it. Without touching the envelope, she held out the drawer and said, "See?"

Chapter 16

Sunday Evening ...

DARREN QUICKLY PUT on gloves and took the envelope from the drawer in Doreen's hands and laid the envelope on the bed. He then took photographs of both sides of the envelope. Even as he did that, his phone rang. "Yeah, Mack, you need to come back here," he said into the phone. She could hear the garbled voice on the other end. "Yeah, she found something. The guys missed it. ... No, I don't know how," Darren said. "An envelope was underneath the night table drawer with Doreen's name on it. I followed standard protocol and snapped photos of the envelope itself, which I'll forward to you. I'm hoping there might be fingerprints or something on it. Yes, I know it'll likely be Rosie's only."

He gave a sideways look at Doreen, who stood here staring at him. "Yes, she's still here, and, of course, she wants to open it. I thought maybe you should come back and deal with this." At that, Doreen fisted her hands on her hips and glared at him. He smirked at her. "Yeah, okay. Talk to you in a few." He hung up and said, "Mack is on his way back."

"The only fingerprints on that," she said, "are Rosie's.

You know that, right?"

"Maybe," he said, "but you know that we'll also check it."

"It'll be another copy of the note she wanted to give to me," she said, crossing her arms over her chest. "May I continue to look?"

He nodded slowly, but he handed her a pair of gloves this time. She snapped them on with a big grin. "And now it feels official." She could hear the others at the doorway. She looked over to see Nan giving her a thumbs-up. Even Richie's grin was broad, and the two of them were crowding out the rest of the seniors from the home. Doreen immediately headed toward the pile on the bed that she'd taken from the night table. She noticed a wealth of chewing gum here. A couple old letters, some medication that looked like pain pills that anybody could get from any drugstore, a couple greeting cards which Doreen opened and studied, then carefully laid to one side. "Did forensics go through here or just the cops who were looking for whatever?"

"Cops looking," he said.

She nodded. "It makes sense."

"It wasn't a crime scene."

"I know that," she said. She kept rifling through the paperwork and found a little address book. She pulled it out, smiling. "I haven't seen one of these in years," she said.

He peered over at her. "I believe they said it was empty."

She flipped through it and nodded. "It is," she said. Except for the very last page, which was a little thick. She studied it carefully and said, "Except these last two pages have stuck together."

"Let me see it," he said.

She handed it to him and headed back to the rest of the

pile. One long letter had been written to someone named Posie. "Nan, does Rosie have a sister named Posie?"

"Yes," Nan said. "What did you find?"

"Rosie wrote out a long letter to her sister, but it was dated a few weeks ago. She never sent it."

Nan just shrugged.

Doreen set it off to the side, wondering why Rosie hadn't mailed it. As Doreen continued to sort through the night table contents, she heard a commotion at the doorway. She could hear Mack's rumble coming toward her. "Now here comes trouble," she muttered.

Darren chuckled. "No help for it," he said. "This is definitely Mack's department."

"Why? Because he's the detective?"

"Well, one of the reasons," he said. "He's also, as we would call it, your handler." At that, he burst out laughing at her.

She glared at him. "That's hardly funny," she said.

"What isn't funny?" Mack asked, as he inched his way between Nan and Richie, neither of whom were willing to give him any room. Mugs however strained forward as if knowing Mack was there to back him up.

Mack came forward to see Darren pointing toward the drawer that had been upended. Mack stared at the envelope, then shook his head and asked, "Why, Doreen?"

"Who knows?" she said eerily. "But obviously she had something she wanted to tell me."

"Maybe," he said. He put on gloves, reached over, and carefully untaped the envelope. And then, with the tape off, they could see the flap wasn't otherwise sealed. They crowded around as he gently pulled the folded page from inside. He opened it up to find an award. "Best Kiwis in the

Garden," he read. "This is dated last year, and it was an award, but it wasn't for Rosie."

Doreen looked at it and asked, "Whose name is on there?"

"I'm not sure," he said. He held it up to the light. "It's really hard to see."

"That'll be Marsha," Nan said. "She won last year."

Doreen turned to look at her. "Won what?"

"Best tropical fruit," she said, as if that completely made sense.

Doreen's frown was instant. "Best of what?

"The contest," Richie said impatiently. "The gardening contest. Everybody knows that we have all these contests for the best flowers and the best veggies, et cetera, et cetera." He punctuated his words with an airy wave of his hand. "Of course, you weren't here last summer, were you?"

Doreen slowly shook her head. "No," she said. "And I haven't seen any advertisements for the contest."

"It's all at the end of the season," Nan said. "And Marsha always wins. Every year she wins."

Everybody turned to stare at the award. "So why does Rosie have this?" Doreen asked.

Nan shrugged. "Who knows?" she said. "But I have to tell you that Rosie's kiwis were something else."

"What kiwis?" Doreen asked, puzzled. "Are you allowed to have your own gardens here?"

"No," Richie said. "However, one designated spot is on the grounds, if you want to plant something, but Rosemoor really doesn't like individual gardens, particularly not veggies."

"What's wrong with veggies?" Doreen asked, frowning. She didn't understand what was going on here, but that letter kept catching her eye. "What were Rosie's kiwis like?"

"Award winners," Richie said. "She had a long history of winning all kinds of awards."

"And she did ask management if she could plant some kiwis on the grounds," Nan said.

"What did management say?" Mack asked, caught up in this discussion despite himself.

Nan gave him a fat smile. "They said no, but she talked to the gardeners, and they said yes."

"So …" Mack encouraged Nan to continue, while he laid the award on the bed.

"Oh, her kiwis weren't here," Nan said.

"She might have been a contender for the award this year?" Doreen asked slowly.

"Rosie's son had established a community garden, years ago, before he died in the crash," Richie said. "But it's full up."

Mack and Doreen exchanged glances. None of this made a whole lot of sense.

Darren even looked at Richie and said, "But then it would be her son's kiwis?"

"Well, he didn't have kiwis in there," Richie said in exasperation. "Keep up, young one."

Darren groaned. Doreen chuckled and Mack grinned. Doreen looked at the award and said, "I'd like a copy of that too, whenever you get around to it, please." And she gave him a fat smile. "It does have my name on it."

Mack glared at her. "It'd be good if you kept out of this," he said.

"It might be good," she said, "but it's not really a workable solution, is it?"

"I'll see," he said in a noncommittal voice.

"In that case," she said, "let me take a picture of it right now." She pulled out her phone and quickly snapped an image of the award as it lay on the bed. Then she looked at him and said, "Now that you're here, you'll stop me from looking around, won't you?" He glared at her. She shrugged and said, "I just want to finish the job." She pointed at the address book Darren held. "Did you find anything with that?"

He shrugged. "Not really," he said. "Could be anything." And he tossed it back into the pile.

She immediately picked it up and studied it again.

"What's wrong with it?" Mack asked.

"Two pages have stuck together," she said.

"But it's empty everywhere else?"

"Yes," she said. She put it off to the side and kept going through the rest of the stuff dumped on the bed from the night table. It was amazing, the bits and pieces that were collected from a life. With that done, she went back to the night table and checked behind it. She even removed everything off the top and checked underneath and inside. She found nothing. But, while she was down here, she checked under the bed. She couldn't really see anything, but Mack and Darren looked at the mattresses and checked between and underneath too.

By the time they were done a good forty minutes later, they had found nothing else of importance here. She nodded and said, "Okay. I'm heading home. Do you mind if I take this little book with me?" She held up the empty one with the stuck pages.

Mack frowned. And then he shrugged and said, "No, that's fine."

"No will, is there?" Nan called from the doorway.

Doreen shook her head. "No will and not even a lawyer's name," she said. "We need to find that for Rosie's sake." And then her gaze landed on the mirror on the opposite wall. She walked over and lifted it off the hook. "Did you guys check behind here?"

"Of course we did," Mack said.

She nodded as she studied the back. "What about inside the backing?"

He came up behind her, and she lifted off the cardboard backing, finding a single piece of paper inside. She held it toward Mack, who immediately snagged the sheet of paper with his gloved fingers and said, "It's her Last Will and Testament. At least that's what it says on here." He checked the date and frowned. "Signed four days ago."

"Good," Doreen said. "That should be at least as authentic as anything."

"Not unless it's signed properly." Darren came up behind her. But, indeed, two witness signatures were on it.

"Now you need to find those people," she said. But her gaze was caught on the actual contents of the will. She pulled out her phone and quickly snapped a picture. Mack turned and glared at her. She shrugged. "You won't let me see it any closer than that, will you?"

"Nope," he said. "This has to all go into the station. We'll contact a lawyer and see what's going on."

"Rosie changed her will at the last minute," Doreen said. "And, given the nasty grandson who was here, I can understand why."

"He's likely to fight it in court," Darren said.

"Unless," Doreen said, "you can find these witnesses. Both of them have typewritten names and not just signatures, so it's probably staff members."

Mack nodded. "I've already got a list coming of all the Rosemoor employees," he said. "We'll talk to them." Then he looked at her and said, "You get to go home now. Besides, it's dark outside. Darren, will you walk her and her animals home, please?"

Darren nodded.

"Right," she said, pulling off her gloves. "My job here is done." And, with a chuckle, she walked toward Nan.

Nan had a massive grin on her face. "I knew you wouldn't let Rosie down," she said. She looked at the mirror. "She stared at that mirror all the time."

"Ha. But I wonder why she would have thought that the will would be found there," Doreen said.

"It probably wasn't something she thought would be found as much as she was hoping that somebody else *wouldn't* find it," Richie said. That made a cryptic kind of sense to Doreen too.

Back home, she and her animals headed straight to bed.

Chapter 17

Monday Early Morning ...

DOREEN WOKE UP the next morning, noting it was Monday. It was hard to believe Sunday had been such a crush of activity. As she laid in bed, she stared up at the ceiling, wondering what the devil that gardening award had to do with anything. Nobody would kill over something like that, and her bet was still on the snotty grandson, Danny. She had quickly checked the photos on her phone when she had gotten in last night, happy to see them, but it was too hard to read the will. And that pissed her off more.

She hopped from her bed and headed downstairs to the kitchen to put on coffee, but she stopped at the back door. She unlocked it and opened it up, then stared in pure joy at her upgraded backyard. But she had to hold the animals back and quickly close the screen door so they didn't jump outside. Because, as much as she wanted her life back in terms of actually using her backyard, she wasn't sure that it was safe to walk on even the deck back there yet, much less the concrete which was still being continuously soaked by sprinklers on timers. She quickly called Mack.

He answered, his voice groggy.

"I'm sorry," she said. "I didn't mean to wake you."

"I'm awake," he said. "And, if I'm not, I have to be anyway, so I can head into work. What's the matter?"

"I don't know if we're allowed to go out the back door now," she said. "The deck, the concrete ..."

He came more awake on that note. "Good question," he said. "I'll say, for the moment, no. Do your best to avoid all of it."

"So we go out the front then today? Because I can't go anywhere otherwise," she said.

"We also have to apply another coat of stain on the wood," he said. "You should be minimizing as much walking around as you can."

"And the concrete?"

"Definitely not for another day, better two," he said.

She groaned. "If you say so," she said, staring out at the lovely backyard and patio. But she couldn't even admire it fully. "I guess I could put them all on leashes and walk around, then come up the creekside, so we can look."

"You could," he said. "But remember that the animals can't walk on the concrete either, so you don't want to take a chance with them getting loose."

"In other words, no walking. Got it," she said. "Okay, I'll need coffee for this then too." And she hung up.

She turned to put on her coffee, knowing the animals wanted to run outside. As soon as she had a cup in her hand, she walked to the front door and called them. There, she let them out in the front yard, walking around a little bit to take a look at what had been done from this angle. On each side of her house, wood blocked access. Comfortable knowing that Mugs and Goliath wouldn't make their way around to the back, she took them for a short walk around the cul-de-sac and down to the creek from that side.

If nothing else, she deserved to have a cup of coffee at her favorite place. Mack was right though. By walking back up to the creek this way, she was putting the deck and all the freshly poured concrete in danger of having the animals walk all over it. When her coffee was gone, she had enough energy to follow the trail to the cul-de-sac and to enter her front door again. She poured herself a second cup of coffee and sat down to some toast and cheese.

Then, with the animals all fed and at her feet, she wondered what today would bring. Yesterday had been nothing but nonstop action. She knew that the men would return somewhere along the line to cart off equipment. And that big pile of gravel in her front driveway would have to be moved too before she needed to drive anywhere because they had dumped it outside her garage door, and her car was inside the garage. She groaned at that. "Good thing I didn't have any plans right now," she muttered.

About an hour and a half later, while she was still doing research into garden contests and basic local fairs held in Kelowna, Nan called. "Good morning, Nan," Doreen said cheerfully.

"Glad you're so bright and cheerful," Nan said. "Goodness. I didn't sleep very well."

"I'm sorry to hear that," Doreen said in a commiserating voice. "It's hard when you have a tough night, isn't it?"

"It so is," she said. "Particularly at this place. Everybody is all abuzz about the new will."

"The trouble is, none of us know what's in it," Doreen answered.

"But you took a picture," Nan said hopefully. "Can't you tell?"

"I meant to download it onto my computer and see if I could blow it up enough to read it," she said. "But right now, I can't see it on my phone at all."

"Well, do it," Nan said, "and then call me back." She hung up.

Realizing what a lousy effect Doreen was having on her normally very polite and proper Nan, Doreen plugged her phone into the computer and downloaded the photos that she'd taken. She opened them up on her laptop, but the will still had pretty horrid lighting. Granted, she had taken the snap quickly before Mack could stop her. Changing the shading ever-so-slightly, she could see that several charities were mentioned and so was Rosemoor. That one was a surprise. So Rosie did have money or assets to pass on? But what she didn't see in there anywhere was any mention of the nasty grandson. She knew Mack would be really pissed if she said anything to anyone about the will, but she wasn't exactly sure what to say to Nan. Just as she figured she should contact Nan, Mack called her back.

"Now that I'm awake," he said, "I did warn you about not sharing any of the information from yesterday. Correct?" And his tone brooked absolutely no argument.

"Nan has already called me this morning," she said, "wondering what was in the will."

"Well, if you tell her, we'll have a problem," Mack said.

"I won't tell her," she said. "Can I tell her what's not in it though?"

"I'd appreciate it if you don't," he said. "Not until we get to the bottom of this. You don't want to cause anybody else to flare up. What if Nan were to go to Danny and say, 'Hi, you're not in the will.' He might retaliate and hurt Nan."

Doreen winced at that. "I guess there's no way to judge the temper of an ill-mannered young pup like that, is there?" she said.

"I'm also still trying to figure out," Mack said, "exactly what Rosie's assets were."

"Good point," she said. "Especially considering she's leaving some of it to Rosemoor."

"Right," he said. "And that's not necessarily unusual, but we have to make sure that nobody at Rosemoor forced her to write that will."

She gasped. "Okay. I won't say anything," she said. "And that's a good point."

"Absolutely it is," he said. "That's why cops are handling this. Remember?" And he hung up.

Chapter 18

Monday Midmorning ...

S EVERAL HOURS LATER—THAT Doreen had spent buried in research—the doorbell rang. She hopped up with Mugs barking like a crazy man, and she scolded him. "What kind of a guard dog are you that we have to wait until they ring the doorbell?" But he wasn't interested in answering her and was simply jumping all over the front door. She opened the wooden door to see one of the guys who had been here on the weekend. "Hey, Harry," she said. "How are you doing?"

"I'm fine," he said. "I got off work early, and I wanted to come see how the deck was doing. I can't walk around because the sidewalk isn't ready for that yet."

She opened the screen door for him and said, "Come on in. We can go through the kitchen, but can we walk on the deck? I haven't even stepped out there yet because I wasn't sure I was allowed to."

He chuckled. "Depends on the coating we put on," he said, "but it was pretty tacky dry last night. It should be more than fine to walk on it now." She led the way through the kitchen to the deck. As soon as the back door was open, he crouched down, reached out, and touched it with his hands. He nodded and immediately stepped on it.

She gasped yet followed him in her bare feet. It was still damp from all the times the concrete had been wetted down. She walked around, admiring the deck and feeling such joy in her heart. "It's absolutely stunning," she said warmly.

"You know what? It's pretty nice," he said with a nod. "We left you some garden space by that patio, once we get the framework off. That'll really make this gorgeous."

"I'm so in love with this," she said, and she couldn't stop beaming. She looked down at the wood. "We have to do a second coat though, I think. Right?"

"Yes," he said. "And it looks like it's ready to be done too."

"But we wear it down with sand first, don't we?"

Harry chuckled. "Indeed, we do. And I don't know if the paint brushes and rollers survived overnight. If they were treated properly, they'll be fine."

She looked at him in surprise and then pointed at the stuff sitting at the bottom of the steps on a board that crossed over the sidewalk. "As far as I know, it's all there."

He walked down to the bottom step and quickly scooped it all up and checked it. "Yeah, it's perfectly good," he said. "Maybe an hour or two hours to do this, max."

"Seriously?" She stared in surprise. "I thought it would take a lot longer."

"The second coat goes on much faster," he said. "You may want a third coat on the top of the railings, although I don't know for sure. It's treated wood anyway." He looked at her. "But I didn't bring any sanders."

"I have some," she said. She led the way through the kitchen to the garage, then flipped on the light switch and watched as he walked to her big workbench.

"Wow," he said, turning in a circle. "I'm seriously impressed. I don't even have this nice a workshop at home."

"I got it from a friend of mine who was moving," she said. "Her husband had passed away, so I recreated exactly the same workshop here. I have a lot of work to do on my home, but I really don't know what I'm doing yet."

He nodded, then picked up two small sanders. At least, she assumed they were. He checked them out, and then he looked at her. "Any chance you have sandpaper?"

She motioned to the set of drawers beside him. "Top drawer."

He opened it up, nodded, and quickly exchanged the old sandpaper for new ones. "Now, how about extension cords?" He looked around on the walls and snagged up two. "Have you ever used one of these sanders?"

"No," she said. "I haven't. But then I've never held a paintbrush in my hand either."

Harry laughed. "Well, it sounds like today's your lucky day." He headed back out to the deck, where he quickly plugged in the sanders and then showed her how to use them. "We're just doing a light pass on the top," he said. "See this board? We haven't done it." And then he turned on the sander and ran it lightly across the top and back again. Then he shut it off and said, "Now feel how smooth it is."

She was amazed. "Wow."

"That's why we do it. It takes off the roughness and allows it to accept a second coat much better," he said. "I'll work on this side. If you've got time right now to give me a hand, maybe we can get it all sanded and a second coat on."

"I'm all for it," she said. And, with her working on the left side—closest to her neighbor, Richard—she kept checking to make sure she was doing it right, swiping her palm over each surface afterward. Next she went to the shorter set of steps here and did the bottom riser first, then the second tier. It didn't take very long. It amazed her how much difference the power sander made for the job. By the time she got one-third of the way through with her side of the deck, Harry was almost done with the rest, meeting up with her. She turned off her sander and asked, "What do we do next?"

"We'll do the railings," he said. "And we still have to do the big steps in the front of the deck."

She went over and did the big steps on the front, while he did the railings. And, before long, they stood, admiring a job well done. He grinned. "And two makes it a much faster job than one," he said.

She nodded and took the sanders back to garage, after banging them lightly to shake off the dust. When she returned, he had the rollers but was looking at her. "I need a cloth," he said. "We have to wipe all the deck down to make sure none of this sawdust from the sanding gets into the next coat."

She raced inside to the kitchen and came back out with two damp cloths. "Will these work?"

"Particularly if they are clean," he said.

She nodded and said, "Clean with warm water."

"Perfect," he said. "We'll rinse them as soon as they get clogged to give it all a nice quick dusting. A shop vac would work too, but I'm not sure that, in this case, it's a good idea."

"I've got a small blower," she said. "Would that work?" And she came out with it.

He quickly took one look at it, smiled, and said, "This is

the reverse of one of those little shop vacuums." He quickly blew off most of the dust, then grabbed the cloth and wiped it down. "This is perfect."

It took them about half an hour, with her running the blower and him wiping. And then, just like that, they were done. "We'll get that second coat on in no time," he said. He took out the can and filled one of the rollers. "I'll use the roller. I want you to take the paintbrush." He demonstrated doing the spindles on the railings. "You take care of all this," he said. "I'll quickly get the base done on the steps and then on the top, so that, by the time you're done, we're on these last few boards up against the kitchen. Okay?" She nodded and went to the far side, then started painting slowly and methodically. She wasn't very good at it, and she wasn't very fast, but she felt a certain pride in doing something herself for her deck. So far, everybody else had done all the work.

"I heard Mack caught another wild case," Harry said.

"Yes. Another dead little old lady," she said sadly. "And this one'll be very much missed."

"Hopefully they all are," he said quietly. "The last thing you want to think about is going to your grave and nobody crying."

"Right," she said. "How sad would that be?"

"I think that would be very terrible," Harry said. "But it's amazing, you know, how many seniors do pass away on a regular basis, and we never hear about them. I'm not even sure what connected these ones in the first place. Except kiwis were tied to each one."

"Probably just the fact that they were found out in a public place," she said.

"Most of the seniors I know passed away in their own beds or in their nursing homes or something like that."

"That makes sense," she said. She straightened up, wincing as she kept trying to get to the spindles underneath the railing. "What about this?" she asked him.

Harry walked over, took a good look, and said, "Good job on the spindles. Now you can put a thicker coat on the tops of the railings, and that may stop us from needing another round." And he showed her how to lay a nice thick bead and then wipe it so it didn't drip. With both of the railings done, she stepped back and stuck the brush into the can, then watched as he finished rolling the stairs and then up onto the big part of the deck. Because he used a roller, his very long strokes went very quickly. He turned and looked at her can and asked, "Do you have any left?"

She nodded. "But not too much. Maybe one-quarter, one-fifth."

He took it from her and poured it into his tray. They were in danger of running out.

"Do we have enough?" she asked worriedly.

"With any luck, yes," he said, and he kept working. And he was two boards short of finishing when he motioned for her to get in the kitchen while she could; then he grabbed the can and, using the brush, scraped out as much as possible and finished up the last two boards from the roller and the brush. When he was done, he stepped backward into the kitchen, smiled, and said, "I wouldn't have wanted to cut that any tighter."

"But it's okay?"

"It's perfect," he said. "And this stain can goes into the recycling." He put his hand inside a nearby plastic bag and tucked the plastic bag inside the can. "Leave it to dry like this," he said. "And then, in a couple days, you'll take that bag out, which should lift all the stain remaining inside, like peeling it off in the hot sun. Then the can goes into the recycling."

"Nice trick." She smiled, then nodded and said, "And the brush?"

"This one you can wash in water," he said. But he looked at the brush and frowned. "It's already losing its bristles."

"Yes, I had a problem with that," she said. "I kept pulling off bristles on the stained surface."

"In that case," he said, "this brush should just go in the trash bin, because, the next time you try to use it, more bristles will loosen." And, with that, he put everything together in another bag. "Not to worry," he said. "I can take this away with me. You don't want the animals to get at it."

"I didn't even offer you any coffee," she said with a laugh.

"Not a problem," he said. "I'm really happy we got that done." He looked at his watch and smiled. "It's my regular time to go home anyway."

"So when do you think I can walk on the deck?" she asked anxiously.

"Not for twenty-four hours for sure," he said, "so no going out there until at least this time tomorrow. By then we'll take the frame off the concrete anyway." And he lifted a hand in goodbye, and, just like that, he was gone. She stood at the open kitchen doorway, trying to block Mugs, who was desperate to go out. She took several photos; then she closed the screen door and locked it. "You can't go out there," she scolded him. "None of us can."

He woofed at her but unhappily.

Chapter 19

Monday Afternoon ...

Doreen sent the photos to Mack and added a text message. **Second coat done.**

She didn't get a response, but then, like he kept trying to tell her, he was busy. She understood that, but it was weird not having him answer quickly. As it was, she was a little bit stuck trying to come up with any more information regarding Rosie's death. But then she had continued her research on kiwis and kiwi contests and kiwi fairs. And, sure enough, this one woman had been winning for years in Kelowna over and over again. Doreen smiled at the thought, then looked up the woman's name to find she was another gray-haired lady. "You better look out because you could be next," she muttered.

And then she realized just how terrible that was of her to say.

"Maybe it's nothing at all," she said. She went back to her work and heard her stomach growling. She still had leftover pizza. She didn't really want any more as she was really craving more vegetables. So she made herself a big salad.

When a pounding came at the front door, she groaned. Mugs was already at the door but acting funny. Instead of barking hysterically, he was whining. Probably Mack was on the outside. She opened the door and found him staring at her. "Normally you just walk in," she said crossly.

"Well, maybe," he said. "I wasn't sure if you were napping or not."

"So pounding on the door was a better way to wake me up?"

"Better than coming in and looming over you, finding you in the living room or somewhere," he said.

She thought about it and said, "Okay. Good point. Did you get my images?"

"Yes," he said. "How did you get that done?"

So she told him about Harry's visit and sanding and painting the deck. He smiled. "And did you have fun doing something yourself?" he asked in a teasing voice.

"Absolutely," she said. "I didn't feel quite so stupid, and it made the deck mine too because I feel like I did something to help."

"And that's a really valid point," he said. "I should have thought of that."

"You can't be expected to think everything," she said, laughing.

His gaze landed on her laptop. "Kiwis?"

"It's research into the contest," she said, "where somebody grows the biggest and juiciest and sweetest kiwis. It's not very common to grow kiwis here, so it's under the tropical fruit category. Besides, I can't let go of the kiwi element in all four of the deaths. I still haven't gotten to the bottom of it. And all the women had kiwis with them. Remember?"

"Are they hard to grow?"

"They need a lot of sunny days, and they're one of those few plants that have males and females," she explained. His eyebrows shot up at that, and she nodded. "Some plants are like that." She motioned at her salad. "I was just making myself something to eat."

"Any pizza left?" he asked, massaging this tummy.

She opened her eyes. "That's why I made a salad," she said. "I wasn't sure I could handle more pizza." He stared at her in surprise. She groaned. "I get it. There's nothing wrong with pizza three times a day, seven days a week, if you're a guy. I happen to like rabbit food too."

He opened the fridge and laughed when he saw two pizza boxes. "So you're not eating any more of this?"

"Oh, I so am," she said. "I thought I'd have some veggies to go with it."

He nodded. "Okay, good enough. Are you sharing?"

"Absolutely," she said, smiling at him. "And they're leftovers anyway."

"Yep, but sometimes," he said, "sometimes, you're a little bit protective of food."

"I don't know about sometimes," she said. "I think that's all the time."

He laughed as he opened the box and pulled out three pieces.

"Don't you want some of the other one too? Isn't it a different kind?" And she pulled out the other box, but he was already warming up those three slices in the microwave.

He looked at it and said, "I'll have that the second time around."

When he opened the back door to the kitchen, she cried out, "Don't."

He turned to look at her and said, "I'm just looking. I won't go out there."

"Good," she said. "I was worried that you'd step on it and leave footprints."

"No," he said, "I wasn't planning on it."

"You have to watch for Mugs too," she said. "He's pretty unimpressed at not having his backyard."

"Makes sense," he said. "After another day, then that should be good."

She nodded. "That's what I was thinking. I asked Harry, and he said at least tomorrow. And hopefully we can take the framework off the bigger slabs of concrete by then too."

"Maybe," he said. "I'll talk to Tony about that."

"Hope so. Watch out for Mugs."

He nodded, but his legs were braced up, and Mugs couldn't squeeze past. Mack finally closed the door, and she let out a sigh of relief. He smiled at her. "Honestly I knew I'm not supposed to go out there."

"I know," she said. "It's nerve-racking though. I can't wait until it's past the danger point."

"You're probably there already now," he said. "I haven't touched it to see if it's dry, but this stuff is amazing with how quickly it sets."

"Well, tomorrow will let us know," she said. "Just have to get through until then." In an effort to change the subject and to keep him away from the deck, she asked, "Any news on Rosie's case?"

"No," he said. "The worst thing about waiting for autopsy results is waiting on the toxicology. If they were given something to simulate a heart attack—of which, yes, I know several drugs are possible—it could take weeks."

"Can you release the bodies in that case?"

"Yes," he said, "we can."

"So have any of the bodies been buried yet?"

"Interestingly enough," he said, "all four had purchased burial plots together at one cemetery."

"Wow," she said. "Me, I want to be cremated."

"What?" he said in a mocking tone. "Don't you want a big monument to Doreen and all her cold cases that she solved, a place where all the tourists can come snapping their cameras all around and taking pictures of your final place of rest?"

She stared at him in horror. "The media taunts me constantly here, now that we're on the Japanese tour bus route," she cried out. "Whoever thought that was a good idea? And why would I want that to continue after I'm dead?"

He chuckled. "No clue." He walked to the kitchen table with his hot pizza and sat down. Then he motioned at the other chair. "You'll join me?"

She added salad dressing to her bowl and cut herself some cheese, which she put on the side of her salad and then walked over with a fork and said, "Yes, I am. But you still haven't told me any results from the related cases yet."

"Nothing to say yet," he said. "So far, there's no motive in anybody killing any of these people."

"They don't all have somebody awaiting their riches?"

"Two of them didn't have any riches," he said. "One was barely surviving, her retirement covering her room costs every month, and we have Rosie, whose assets we're still working to track down based solely on her will made just days ago. We did find her lawyer though, so he's on it."

"Oh, good," she said. "Speaking of lawyers ..."

He nodded. "Remember? My brother's supposed to come next weekend," he said.

She wrinkled up her face. "It'd be really nice if I could miss that visit."

"You can't," he said, a hard note entering his voice. "No way you can. We need to get to the bottom of this. And, at least, he'll tell us what he's found so far."

"Yep," she said. "Not exactly a highlight of my life."

"Look at how much more exciting your life is now," he said.

"It's much more exciting." She nodded with a big smile. "But how sad too because it reminds me of what I didn't have for a life before now."

"You can't keep focusing on the past," he said. "Maybe that's a problem with you doing cold cases. All you're doing is spending so much time looking at history."

"Which is why," she said with a big smile, "I'd be happy to help you with your current case." He glared at her. "And then there's the fact that Rosie's husband just got up and walked away out of the blue. To never be heard from again."

Mack, lifting a big piece of pizza with two hands, stopped and stared at her.

"Or did you not hear about that?"

"Tell me," he commanded.

She shrugged and said, "I don't really have too many details. But apparently her husband disappeared about ten years ago."

"Interesting," he said. "Was it ever reported to the police?"

"I don't know," she said. "Mack, was it ever reported to the police?" She wiggled her eyebrows at him. "If anybody would know, it's you."

"I'd have to look in the files. But nothing popped up when we started a file on her," he said, as he munched his way through the hot pizza. His gaze had shifted to the backyard, as if contemplating how this would impact the mystery. "I wonder if she ever declared him dead either? Maybe the Last Will and Testament will be completely tied up with this missing person angle on her husband. After all, barring a valid will, I would presume her estate would go to him, if he's alive and if they are still married. Or did this grandson know anything about his granddad?"

"Hard to say," she said, as she munched on her salad. "Is anybody even talking to him?"

"I had a talk with him this morning."

"How fun was that?"

"Not," he said. "He's not saying anything, except that he has full rights to everything."

"Did you tell him about the will?"

"No, not yet," he said. "That's up to the lawyer who handles her estate."

"And so will that new will be honored?" she asked worriedly.

"Again, that's up to us to help the lawyer settle that issue," he said.

"Meaning, you won't tell me if you found the witnesses and spoke to them yet?"

"No, I'm not telling you," he said cheerfully.

She glared at him. "Mack, you have a mean streak."

At that, he burst out laughing. "Maybe," he said, "but some things just can't be released."

"Great," she said. "That's not fair, you know?"

"It is what it is," he said.

And, with that, she had to be satisfied.

Chapter 20

Tuesday Morning ...

TUESDAY MORNING, DOREEN woke up to an odd sound. She glanced at her watch and realized it was seven o'clock already. She bounced from her bed and peered out the window to see a couple men in her backyard. Gasping, she quickly dressed and, with Mugs in tow and Goliath completely ignoring her, stretching out in the bed instead, and Thaddeus squawking on her shoulder, she ran down the stairs.

She opened the wooden kitchen door and called out through the screen door, "Good morning."

Tony looked up, smiled, and waved a hand.

"I don't know if the deck's safe to walk on. Is it?" she asked.

He walked over and asked, "When did you paint it?"

"Yesterday midmorning," she said, "maybe a little later."

Both the men looked and nodded. "It's fine to walk on," he said, "so you can come out. We're here to check on the concrete itself."

She clipped on Mug's leash, then opened the screen door and stepped out onto the deck with him. She just loved the fact that she had this beautiful wooden deck now. "It's gorgeous."

"Don't put any of the furniture up there yet," Tony said. "It'll need a little bit longer to set. You can walk on it, but don't plan to put the table and chairs back yet. They'll scrape through that coating pretty fast."

"Until when?"

"Tomorrow morning will probably be fine," he said. "Honestly, even later this afternoon will be fine. But it's just that you'll always want to give everything a final twenty-four hours to harden up."

She nodded, excited to be walking here, especially with Mugs, who was sniffing the wood intently. "And what about the concrete?"

"All the framework can come off," he said. "I don't start work until ten this morning, so I thought I'd come early and do this now, so you had access to your backyard. My buddy here, Brody, has a pickup, and he wants the wood afterward."

She looked at Brody, who wasn't even watching her. He was measuring off the wood. "What's he using it for?"

"Same thing," Brody said. "Once it's stained with concrete, you can't use it for anything else."

"I guess you could if you chipped it all off and sanded it down," she said.

Both men laughed. "Wood like this is cheap," he said. "To do that takes a ton of work."

She nodded and didn't know what else to say but figured that Mack would know. She said, "I'll go inside and put on some coffee. I hate to admit it, but I slept in this morning."

"Go," Tony said. "Do your thing."

So she went in and put on coffee, then quickly texted

Mack. When the phone rang, she figured she hadn't explained herself. "Sorry, Mack," she said. "I was trying to figure out if that's normal."

"What part of what is normal?" he asked, his tone all business.

"That the wood will be handed off to somebody else," she said in a whisper.

"Wood used to frame concrete is often done that way," he said. "As long as it's pretty smooth, it can be reused to frame up another pouring of concrete. For the rounded patio we used hard plastic edging that with rebar to keep the shape we wanted. The wood forms, the plastic edging, and the rebar can all be reused. Tony supplied a lot of that wood anyway. You didn't, so it's perfectly good to pass it along."

She smiled with relief. "Thanks," she said. "I didn't want to seem like I was really cheap, when they'd done so much work. I just wasn't sure if we needed the wood still."

"Nope," he said. "And, even better, you won't have to pay for a dump run."

She gasped in joy. "Oh my," she said. "I didn't even think of that."

"Right," he said, "so this is working out all that much better for you."

"Okay," she said. "In that case, I guess I should offer them coffee, huh?"

"I would," he said. "You never know when you might need their help again." And he hung up.

She pocketed her phone and opened the kitchen door. She could leave it open now, and Mugs wasn't making too much of an attempt to go down to the concrete. It must have smelled funny to him. She looked for the two guys, but they had disappeared. She went through the garage, opened the big door out front, and saw a pickup parked there. The men were loading up the wood. "Hey, did you guys want coffee?" she asked.

Both of them shook their heads. "No, we're on a tight time frame," Tony said. "We'll pop off all this framework, load it up, and get out of your hair."

"Thank you so much for all your help. I just love how my backyard looks now," she said. She was still in bare feet and couldn't walk around the side because of the gravel in the front that she didn't want to step on.

"It's looking really good," Brody said. "He did a great job."

"Everybody did," she said. She made her way back into the house, then poured herself a cup of coffee and stepped onto her new deck, watching with glee as the men pounded and slammed the framework apart. They collected all the wood, and she hoped a ton of nails or screws wouldn't be left behind in her yard.

When Tony looked up, noting her bare feet, he said, "You may want to take a walk around in sturdy shoes afterward. We're doing the best we can to make sure no nails pop free, but it's always possible we've missed some."

"That's a good idea," she said. "As soon as you're done with one section, I'll come take a closer look."

"Did the captain ever come back with the framework to put up that gate?"

She looked at him in surprise. "Honestly I forgot all about it," she said. "But I presume not, because it wasn't there when I was looking yesterday."

"Maybe I'll finish that off on the weekend," Tony said. "And you also need a gate on this side."

"That would be good," she said. "I wouldn't have to

worry about Mugs running out onto the road."

"It doesn't help with the creekside much," he said, looking back at the creek. "But then, if he's a smart dog, he won't be going into that rushing water anyway."

She glanced to see the creek was, indeed, much higher than she had expected. "No," she said with a smile. "He loves the water, but he does have smarts enough to stay out of it."

"Right," he said with a smile. "We shouldn't have too much more to do here. It's going pretty fast."

And, even as she looked on, his buddy Brody walked down with a sledgehammer, releasing the framework all the way down on one side to the creek and then hitting it all the way back. Tony quickly grabbed the freed-up wood and collected an easy half-dozen pieces, then carried them out to the truck in the front. Three trips each and all the wood was collected on the side, and Brody was already working around to the other side. "Is it safe to walk on the paths now?" she asked, when Tony came around.

He immediately hopped onto the concrete and said, "Absolutely."

She grinned and hopped down with Mugs at her side. "Wow," she said. "I'm absolutely loving it. This is wonderful."

"Looks pretty good, doesn't it?" he said. "The colors are a little darker on the patio, but it should balance out pretty quickly."

She had noticed the color variation but hadn't cared enough to even make a comment about it. "This is a stunning backyard now," she said.

"When you get the gardens fixed up just the way you want them," he said, "it really will be quite an oasis for you."

She looked over at her gardens. "I've got a lot of plants filled in on one side but not the other yet."

"Not a problem," he said. "This town is garden crazy. I'm sure you will have no problem getting in more plants."

"I was wondering about putting some vegetables in," she admitted. "I haven't done any vegetable gardening before, but it sounds like fun." She watched as Brody walked up again with a sledgehammer and started doing the sidewalk on the right-hand side. And very quickly, Tony was behind him, picking up the loose boards. She followed them out slowly as they made the last of their trips, and she realized the entire side of the house now had a beautiful path, and she wouldn't have to worry about weeds or mowing or anything. She stood in the front, where the grass and the concrete stopped and grinned. "This is gorgeous," she said. "Of course I have lots of gravel to dump, but that's all right too."

"You shouldn't have too much of a problem with that," he said. "Just along the sides to fill it in a bit."

"I got this."

The men hesitated; then they looked at their watches and said, "We wanted to put the gravel in place, but we're late."

She waved them off. "Go, go, go," she said. "I can get at that on my own time."

"If you're sure?" Brody asked.

She smiled and nodded. "It'll be fine," she said. As they disappeared, she thought it wouldn't be fine. That was a lot of gravel to move. But then nobody said she had to do it all at once. She also wondered if she should put something underneath it to help stop the weeds. She knew nothing would ever completely stop the tenacious weeds. She headed back inside and texted Mack. **They've finished the concrete too. I'll send you some photos.** After that she quickly took a bunch of photos, and sent them to Mack. And then, with Mugs and Goliath and Thaddeus squawking, she walked along the sidewalks. Her brand-new, beautifully accented sidewalks went all the way down to the creek. She knew Tony had said something about the high water in the creek, but she noted the water from the creek would have to rise two feet before it hit her concrete. She smiled as she stood here in a little bit of the pathway. The animals were at her side, and she said, "You know what? This is a perfect place to sit." And she plunked her butt down on her new bench and crossed her legs out in front of her. She took a selfie at that point in time, laughing as the sidewalk behind her stretched all the way beyond her, and she sent it to Nan. When Nan called her a few minutes later, she was ecstatic.

"Oh my," she said. "That looks divine. May I come up and visit?"

"Of course," Doreen said, laughing. "You know you don't have to ask under normal circumstances, but as long as I know you're coming, I guess it's okay for you to walk here alone."

"Can I still walk along the path?"

Doreen hopped up, looked at the creekside, and said, "It's narrower, but I think you can still come up quite fine."

"Okay, I'll be there in ten minutes then," Nan said.

"I'll watch for you." Doreen chuckled. "Any other reason why you're in such a hurry?"

"Yep," she said. "I have information."

"Okay," Doreen said. "I'm waiting outside, right at the creek."

"Be there in five then." And she hung up.

It was time to answer a call from Mack, who was astonished that the guys had already taken the framework off.

"They did ask if the captain was doing a frame for the one gate for me too," she said.

"He hasn't mentioned it," Mack said. "I'll ask him about it. I remember hearing him talk about it."

"Yes," she said. "But you know what? I totally forgot about it myself."

She hung up from the call with Mack to see Nan turning the corner at the far end. Mugs took off like a dirty streak, his ears flapping in the wind as he raced toward Nan. She stopped and chuckled as Mugs wove through her legs at his joy in seeing her. Goliath, not to be outdone, sauntered toward her with that casual elegance of a cat that said *I'll meet you halfway, but you'll have to come the rest of the way.* And he stopped, sure enough, halfway. Nan walked toward him and bent down, then scooped the big guy up in her arms and gave him a cuddle. As she walked toward Doreen, Thaddeus said, "Nan is here. Nan is here."

Nan chuckled and reached out a hand, and Thaddeus hopped up onto the back of her hand and walked up her arm. When he got there, he said, "Thaddeus loves Nan. Thaddeus loves Nan."

Doreen's heart melted as she watched Nan and Thaddeus cuddle close, both with their heads together and their eyes closed, enjoying the moment.

"I'm so delighted to see his vocabulary is increasing," Nan said.

"As long as it's all nice things," Doreen said with a smile.

She hopped up and gave Nan a gentle hug. "What do you think?" She pointed to her backyard.

Nan stopped and stared. "I can't believe how much

172

you've done," she cried out in shock. "You've only been in the house for what, not even three months?"

"It feels like much longer," Doreen said. "But I think it has been three months, maybe a day or two short."

"It's absolutely stunning." Nan looked at the sidewalk and asked, "Can we step on it?"

"Yep, it's safe now. It's all dried."

As they walked along the sidewalk, Doreen said, "I think I'll probably put gravel in along here, so I can run the lawnmower across and not have to worry about it."

"That would look real nice," Nan said. "Anything that makes life easy works for me."

"That's how I feel," she said.

When they got to the big patio, Nan stopped and stared. "Never even occurred to me," she said, "to put in a patio like this. It's absolutely gorgeous." Nan walked up the stairs. And using the railing, she hopped up on the big deck and stared, her jaw dropping. "This should have been here a long time ago. You have done a phenomenal job."

"Not me," Doreen said. "Honestly it was mostly Mack and his teammates."

"Well, it's good," she said, "because you've helped them lots. It's great that you gave them an opportunity to help back."

"I hadn't considered it that way," Doreen said thoughtfully. "I was just thinking they were helping me."

"Yes, they were," Nan said. "But it's important for people to have an outlet to give back as well. You don't want anything to be too one-sided. It starts to make you feel bad after a while." She raced down the steps, walked around the sidewalk, came back up the next set of steps, and repeated it again. She laughed. "I feel like a little kid," she said. "This is just beautiful."

"I know," Doreen said with a big and happy sigh. "I'm seriously happy about this."

"You should be," she said. "And how much did it cost you?"

Doreen gave Nan a big, fat smile. "Nothing," she said. "Absolutely nothing. Well, some screws and then beer and pizza in multiple man-serving amounts on two days."

As Doreen looked around, Tony had taken the concrete mixer and all the rest of his stuff with him too. "They even cleaned it up afterward, and the framework was going to another job, so I don't have any of that left to force me into a dump run." She frowned and said, "A little bit of wood was unused." And she turned around and pointed. "Two boards were sitting off to that side. I think that's all that's left though of the good wood. We still have to get rid of the old deck."

Nan stared. "This is unbelievable," she murmured. She looked at Doreen, and tears were in her eyes. "You know what? It never occurred to me to *not* give you the house," she said, "but now that I have given it to you and have seen what you've done with the backyard, I realize just how right I was to do this."

Chapter 21

Tuesday Late Morning...

DOREEN IMMEDIATELY GAVE Nan a hug. "Honestly," Doreen said, "I'm so happy you did. It's giving me more sense of home than all those years I was married."

"And I think being home is what's really important. It doesn't matter where it is. Home is where the heart is, and this, for you, is now where you belong," Nan said. "And I couldn't be happier." She looked around and smiled. "So, do we get a cup of tea, and can we sit out here?"

"I don't think any furniture is allowed on the wood deck yet," she said, "but we can probably put the table on the patio. Let me go put on the kettle." She bounded up the steps and into the kitchen. As she came outside again, Nan pulled something from the roomy pocket of her sweater and handed it to her. "What's this?"

"Banana bread," she said. "I can't remember who made it for me, but I get so much of this stuff at Rosemoor that I just can't possibly eat it all."

"Well, I can't hardly argue with that," Doreen said. "I'll be happy to have a cup of tea with a piece. I still have zucchini bread from Millicent as well if you'd like a piece."

"Good, keep it," Nan said. "More than enough is there for tea for us for now." She continuously walked around, smiling. "This is truly brilliant."

"Come around here," Doreen said. And she showed her both sides of the house.

"Now, this is perfect. And, yes, you need the added gravel. With that, you'll have all this nice and tidy."

As she walked out to the side where anybody would travel through the garage and around the house, she said, "We'll put the gates in here. And then look." She pointed to the pile of gravel in the driveway. "I'll move all this around and fill in the edges."

Nan stared at her in surprise. "It's so perfect," she said, as she turned around to look. "You've really added value to the house."

"But I don't have any intention of selling," she said comfortably. "I'm too happy to have a home."

"And I love hearing that," she said. The two women moved inside to make the tea; then Doreen told Nan to wait and give her time to move her little outdoor table and chairs to her new patio. That done, Doreen returned and carried the teapot and the banana bread to the table, while Nan carried a tray with cups and plates. She and Nan set up there to have their treat.

Nan sat with her face up to the morning sun and said, "What a beautiful morning. Too bad Rosie isn't here to enjoy it."

"I know," Doreen said. "And we don't have anything to go on as to why these women have dropped dead."

"There's always something," she said.

"I know, but none of them had any great wealth that the relatives would want. Yet two of the families were arguing or fighting with Rosie and Delilah."

Nan nodded. "I did find out a little bit more."

"About Rosie?"

"Yes," she said. "Apparently her husband might be still alive."

"What?" she said. "Did Rosie tell you that?"

"Danny was there again today," Nan said in a derogatory tone. "He was trying to get back into Rosie's room. I asked him what he was looking for, and he said a will. I didn't tell him anything. I wanted him to stew about it all."

"Right," Doreen said, thinking about that. "It depends. He thinks he's getting an estate."

"And that's what I can't understand," Nan said. "It's not like she had any money. I mean, we do keep ourselves quite tight at the place, and she had enough money to go out for lunch and her basics, but she never talked about having any money problems. But then, a lot of women wouldn't talk about having money or not having money," Nan said. "It's not ladylike. In her case though, she took it to the extreme."

"Do you think she was hiding something?"

"I don't think so," she said. "But I do wonder if she doesn't own something that we didn't know about."

"I'm sure she did," Doreen said. "She was a friend, but that doesn't mean she'd talk about everything that she owned, would she?"

"No, and she did place reasonable bets. She was never a big gambler, and she was always fairly prudent. She put her winnings off to the side and kept playing with a sealed mouth," Nan said with approval. "That's always somebody who understands how money works."

"Then it's up to the lawyer to figure out what she has for stocks and bonds," Doreen said. "For all you know, she owned real estate in town too."

"It's quite possible," Nan said. "We'll have to wait and see."

"Is that the news you wanted to tell me about?"

"Yes," Nan said. "And the fact that the contest is run by one of the daughters of someone at Rosemoor."

"What contest?" Doreen asked, struggling to shift conversations. "What are you talking about?"

"She's organizing the judging at the local fair this August," she said.

"Is she a new person to run it?"

"No, she's run it every year for the last ten or so years."

"Wait a minute." Doreen got up, walked into the house, grabbed a notepad and pen, came back, and said, "Who is this person?"

"Candace Ethrembel," Nan said, pronouncing it slowly. "Her mother, Gladys, has been here forever."

"Okay," she said. "And she's looked after the local fair for what, a dozen years?"

"Something like that."

"And I'm to contact her why?"

"Oh my," Nan said. "I didn't say you had to contact her."

Doreen looked up at her grandmother and then back down at her notes. "Okay," she said. "And yet you must have a reason for why you brought it up."

"Sure," she said. "Just in case you wanted to follow up on that award for the kiwis."

"I need to do some research on growing kiwis in town anyway," Doreen said.

"I only know of two who can."

"Can what?"

"Grow kiwis," Nan said, frowning at her. "Are you really missing a bunch here?"

"No," Doreen said. "I'm trying to figure out what it is that you're trying to tell me without telling me."

Nan's frown deepened. She reached across and patted her hand, then said, "Obviously it's been a very busy weekend. I think you need a break."

Doreen nodded. "You're right. It's been a busy weekend. And it's now Tuesday, and I'm not even sure what's on my agenda this week, except that I'll move that gravel first because I can't go anywhere until it's gone from my driveway."

Nan thought about that for a moment and then chuckled. "I guess they didn't think about that when they left it there, did they?"

"I think that wasn't a top priority for them at the time," she said. "You should have seen it. I swear we had close to a dozen men here."

"I believe it," Nan said. "It's that old community spirit we used to have but seems to have been lost for a long time now."

"Right," she said.

"But I'm really glad that you managed to find that spirit again."

"Me too," Doreen said.

As soon as Nan was gone, Doreen looked at the name on her pad of paper and then looked up a phone number. She should have checked with Nan for one, but she hadn't offered it to her and was acting so odd about this whole conversation. Better that Doreen found the number herself. Apparently there was even a website, and who knew there was a Kelowna fair in the first place? Doreen got a hold of one of the organizers, who then passed on the number for Candace. When Doreen got a hold of Candace, she was quite affable and cheerful about the whole fair-festival contest thing.

"I arrange for the judges in each category," she said. "And honestly the competition is quite fierce."

"Meaning that a lot of really high-end gardeners are in town?" Doreen asked in surprise.

"Absolutely, and they're all very protective of their methodologies and the little tricks and tips that they have," she said with a laugh. "Now the tomatoes are always a big fight because it's hard to judge the flavor of a tomato. Everybody's got their own special things that they like, whether it's robust or juicy or firm or fleshy. You know? There's just so many different characteristics. So we generally do it by size. The same thing goes for the largest pumpkins. We have the largest zucchinis contest. We have the largest squashes contest. And, of course, now they're doing megacarrots too, so we have the longest carrots with the best tone and color. It's all very competitive. You don't realize how much people get into this until you join something like this event and realize it's serious business for them."

"Right," Doreen said. "That's amazing. Even tropical plants?"

"That's always been a bit of a difficult one," she said, "because what constitutes a tropical plant? We had a list, and then the list kept expanding, as people would say, I'm growing this or I'm growing that. So it's pretty wide open, and it does cause a bit of kerfuffle at the end of the day."

"And yet I understand somebody with kiwis has won every time?"

"Indeed," Candace said. "And you have to admit, with

kiwis, you can grow them down on the coast, but we have kiwis, passion fruit, bananas ..." And her voice trailed off as she was lost in thought. "I can't remember the list of acceptable fruits," she said. "But the kiwis have been the biggest, roundest, juiciest, and sweetest fruits you can imagine," she said enthusiastically. "Also the most contentious winners in any category."

"But isn't that like comparing apples to oranges?" Doreen asked in confusion.

"And we've had that argument several times," the woman said with a heavy sigh. "And again, the contenders get quite irate about it. So we made it very clear that these were the fruits that could be entered, and then they had to go up against each other."

"Well, I guess it's fair, as long as people understand what they're up against," Doreen said, wondering how anybody would find any of this comfortable to deal with.

"Well, it doesn't matter if it's fair or not," she said. "We do the best we can, but there will always be dissenters."

"Has anybody ever said the kiwi winner wasn't fair?"

"Absolutely," she said. "All the time. It's quite irritating too because we have this point-counting system, where it's judged by its color and its size comparative to, you know, kiwis growing in its own native country, blah, blah, blah. But honestly, so far, Marsha Langford has done an absolutely lovely job with those kiwis. She gets premium price for them, and, every year, she keeps winning."

"Has anybody else been close?"

"Yes, yes, of course. We've had a couple passion fruits that have been grown in greenhouses, but then they were disqualified because of that," she said apologetically. "We make it very clear that this isn't a greenhouse competition because that changes things completely."

Doreen frowned, trying to figure out how that would change anything. "So, it has to be grown out of doors, and that's about it?"

"Out-of-doors locally and you can start it from a seed indoors. You can start it in a greenhouse too, but it has to be moved outside," the woman said. "We do have a list on the website if you're that interested."

"Well, it is interesting," she said. "I understand Rosie was one of the kiwi fanatics."

"Well, the problem is, once Marsha won all the kiwi contests for a couple years, everybody else tried to grow kiwis too. Some people were calling her a cheat and things like that," she said. "And it did get pretty ugly last year."

"How could she have cheated?"

"Well, that was one of the things that the judges were confused about. But apparently the argument was that she had grown them in large pots and then had kept them in the greenhouse well past the point that they were allowed, and, by the time she moved them out for the competition, they'd already come to the fruiting stage, and so it was cheating."

"And yet did you guys check that out?"

"Well, not really," she said. "This is supposed to be all in fun, and, of course, the minute you start having winners, you end up having losers. And, in this case, it ended up being sore losers."

"And how were they sore losers?"

"Well, they had kiwis," she said, "but they weren't anywhere near as fat and as plump as the ones the winner had."

"Right. So then professional jealousy kicks in," Doreen said, having seen it many times before. "And they knocked the winner?"

"Exactly," Candace said. "I'm glad you understand."

"Well, unfortunately for Rosie, she can't enter this year."

"I did hear that she passed away," Candace said. "And that's very sad. It is a problem though, when we have such an elderly selection of contestants."

"Is it mostly a popular contest for seniors?"

"All ages get into it," she said. "We do have a few in their thirties, several in their forties and fifties, but honestly the seniors in their sixties and seventies are really, really strong advocates of this fair. And they love the contests. And we do have, you know, like pie-baking contests and cake-baking contests and a jam contest. There are a lot of contests. So honestly, the tropical fruit, although it's an oddity and it's a fun contest, is only one of about forty, I think."

"Wow," Doreen said. "That puts a lot of pressure on you to keep a lot of judges moving through the fair."

"Every year it's a challenge," she admitted. "There's no easy way to get people in to do this. Nobody wants to pick a winner because, like I said, there's always a loser then."

"Do you ever have just one or two entries?"

"A couple times we've only had two entries in some categories," she said, "but it's never happened that we've just had one."

"Good to know," she said. "And, yeah, I was looking into Rosie's life. I understand that she had some secret weapon for her kiwis this year, so to know that she can't enter them now was just sad. I wondered if it would upset the applecart at all."

"Well, I'll tell you this. She is one who registered a complaint last year against Marsha. She and Delilah."

"Delilah Norstrom?" Doreen asked, remembering the name of one of the other dead women.

"Yes, that's her. The two of them were quite upset,"

Candace said. "They were pretty positive that Marsha was growing the kiwis in the greenhouse."

"They are climbers too, aren't they?" Inside a growing suspicion brewed.

"Exactly," Candace said. "And they're big. Plus you need male and female plants."

"Right," she said. "So, unless somebody digs it up and sees a pot-bound root ball was at the base of the kiwis, there's really no way to know if they had come from pots or not."

"And again, this is all in fun," Candace said, "so we try hard not to get into something like that. But we do take the accusation seriously."

"And what did you do about it?"

"Well, what we did was talk to Marsha and ask her about it and said that there were concerns from other contestants."

"What did Marsha say?"

"She was adamant that she hadn't cheated," Candace said. "And really, again, we had to take her word for it."

"And, of course, if she's won consistently, then that's even a bigger problem," Doreen said, nodding. "What was Marsha's last name?"

"Langford, Marsha Langford," she said. "For a while there, she was entering a lot of different contests. But the only one she ever really did well in was the tropical fruits."

"Perfect," Doreen said. "That's always good to know."

"Right," she said. "Anyway, I've got to run. If you're interested in entering, check out the website. We have bulbs, perennials, and annuals too. We have all kinds of categories. And that keeps changing too, so, if you don't find anything this year, take a look later, and maybe you'll find something that you can win at next year."

And, with that, the other lady hung up.

Chapter 22

Tuesday Lunchtime ...

DOREEN COULDN'T HELP herself. She had to look up where this Marsha Langford person lived. It was noted that she'd entered one of the contests for a beautiful garden too. With that distinction, her address was clearly printed on the contest website. Doreen didn't know if Marsha still lived there. But, hey, it was worth a walk. She pulled it up on Google and smiled. It was just past where Heidi's house was, around a corner. Doreen could avoid Heidi's house if she wanted to, or she could carry on another couple blocks.

Now was a perfect afternoon to go. She should be moving gravel, but she wouldn't do that just yet. She made herself an omelet first and sat down on her brand-new patio, even though she was not too hungry after the banana bread. But it could be hours before she ate again. So, with the omelet tucked inside her belly, nice and warm and happy, she headed out with all the critters.

As soon as she got to Heidi's, Mugs got excited. Doreen walked past Heidi's, knowing that the woman wouldn't be out in the garden. Although Aretha might. But Doreen carried on down past them, took a right, and then a left. Sure enough, she was where this Marsha Langford lived—or maybe used to. Doreen walked past the property to see the front garden in a blooming array of chaos. Mugs immediately sniffed the ground, his tail wagging at the fresh garden.

She stopped and smiled because it was gorgeous. Not the same controlled look as Heidi's, but it was a garden where somebody had tried a little too enthusiastically to grow a bunch of flowers and then had walked away. While she wasn't looking, the flowers had taken off and grew without any help from a human. It was a colorful battle as each plant tried to fight with the other.

A woman popped her head over the top and said, "Hello."

Mugs woofed, backing up slightly. Doreen smiled and said, "Hi. I had to stop and admire the chaos."

"Isn't that a good word for it?" the woman said. "I'm Marsha, by the way. Some people still come by to take a look at this, after I became a semifinalist in one of the garden contests," she said proudly.

"I was talking to Candace about the county fair judging contests," Doreen said. "And she mentioned that you were active in them."

"Yes, I've been the steady winner of the kiwi contest for years now," the woman said with a big smile. "Of course those take a lot of work."

Doreen studied her and guessed she had to be in her mid-to-late seventies. "Kiwis are an interesting fruit to grow here," she said. "I never would have guessed."

"Oh, they do quite well," she said. "Of course, they have to be indoors over winter. The rules allow them to be in a greenhouse over winter, but you have to have them out in the garden by their stated date. Still I've managed to make it work."

"If you say so," Doreen said. "I have a lot more experience with perennials than I do fruits."

"Well, kiwis, they really have to be babied," she said. "I do have a bunch of plants in the back, but I keep a very tight rein on who gets to come in and out because I don't want anybody to steal my secrets."

Doreen couldn't help but wonder what secrets one would have that had anything to do with growing kiwis. "Is the contest that ferocious?"

"Oh my, yes," Marsha said with a big smile. "A certain amount of cash is involved in winning the awards, but, once you do win, it's way worse because you have to keep winning."

"But it's all in good fun, isn't it?" Doreen said cautiously. Mugs walked towards her then laid down on the cement. Goliath flumped beside him. Apparently, they'd had enough of this spot. Or maybe they wanted to have a long nap here. The vagaries of her animals was something she still didn't understand. Thaddeus appeared to be snoring gently at her neck too.

"Well, of course it's in good fun. ... But it's really not in good fun. I mean," she said, "it's a contest. And some people are deadly competitive."

At the term *deadly competitive*, Doreen winced. "Because, of course, it was competitive for some and deadly for others. I hear Rosie would have something that would give you a better run for your money," she said with a smile.

At that, Marsha snorted. "No," she said. "No way she was because it was not possible. I'm definitely by far the better kiwi grower."

"Ah," she said in a more conciliatory tone seeing Mugs

now on his feet and glaring at Marsha. "Well, I understood that she had some kiwis growing here in a community garden that would supposedly outdo yours."

The woman waved her hand at her. "People have been saying that for a long time," she said. "But it's absolutely not possible. My kiwis are stupendous."

"Of course I can't see them, can I?" she said.

Marsha gave her a fat smile and said, "Nope."

"Ah," Doreen said. "Okay then." She could see the greenhouse around the side of the house. "And I see you've got quite a good-size greenhouse too."

"Absolutely."

She smiled, then she waved her hand at the garden of flowers. "This is truly beautiful too."

"Thank you," she said. "I was thinking about entering the contest again."

"Do you know who your competitors are before you go into each contest?"

"No," she said, "not always. There're the usual suspects, and that's how I know that I'll win the kiwis again though. And, of course, I should because I've got the better plants."

"Do you grow the kiwis and keep the seeds?" she asked curiously.

"I do," she said. "However, sometimes the next-generation seeds aren't as good."

"Right," Doreen said with a nod. "Has anybody ever come close?"

"Rosie did last year," the woman said with a sniff. "I was pretty sure she was cheating."

At that, Doreen's eyebrows rose. "How does one cheat?"

The woman lowered her voice and leaned forward. "Greenhouse work," she said. "Too much greenhousing time. They do not allow us to have greenhouse plants in the contest. There are hardy kiwi varieties but they produce really tiny fruit so this way, being judged by size, we have to grow the normal varieties to be competitive."

"Which, I guess, considering kiwis are tropical, would make it even more of a challenge."

"Would it ever," the woman said with her eye roll. "You have to baby them and watch the summer nights in the spring and the dead heat in the summer."

"Right," Doreen said with an all-knowing nod. But inside, she was trying to figure out how would anybody maintain the temperature when it was so variable here. Kelowna did get a lot of days where it could be 40 degrees or in the high 30s for weeks on end, but that wasn't exactly tropical weather either. And sometimes it would be 25 degrees Celsius every day for a whole month in August. That was not tropical in any way. "Well, I'll be excited to see how you do this year."

"I'll win," the woman said without question in her voice.

"Nice to be so confident," she said. "Did you hear what happened to Rosie though?"

"No," she said, stabbing her rake in the ground. "What happened?"

"Oh, dear," Doreen said. "Maybe I shouldn't tell you. Or, at least I should tell you, but I'm sorry. It might upset you. She passed away Sunday morning."

The woman looked at her in shock. "Seriously?"

"Yes," she said, "seriously."

"Well, that's too bad," she said slowly. "Rosie was the only one who could give me a run for my money."

"I'm sorry," Doreen said. "I guess it does help to do better when you realize that you are challenged by a competitor."

"Competition is healthy," Marsha said, staring off in the distance. "I heard that a couple other women had passed away, who were involved in the contest too, but they were never really viable contestants."

At that, Doreen turned to look at her. She listed the names of the four women.

Marsha nodded. "They were all in the same contest, you know?"

"Wow," Doreen said with a smile. "Apparently growing kiwis is deadly."

The woman laughed. "Oh my," she said. "That's really funny. But, no, I'm not worried. In my world, kiwis are a lifesaver and not a killer."

"Why is that?"

The woman paused, and a small smile played around her lips. "Because I was more or less dead inside, until I started growing kiwis," she said. "Something about that plant clicked with me, and I perked right up. I lost my husband a good ten years ago, and I was pretty depressed about it."

"I'm sure," Doreen said with a nod. "How did he die?"

"He just up and disappeared one day," the woman said in a shocking announcement to Doreen. Marsha's phone rang at that time. She looked up at Doreen and said, "Sorry, but I've got to answer this." She had her phone at her ear as she walked toward the front steps into her house, leaving Doreen standing in shock.

Chapter 23

Tuesday Afternoon ...

DOREEN HEADED OFF in a daze. She was struggling to believe what she just learned. She needed more information, but it was obviously not the right time. As she watched, her own phone rang. She looked to see it was Mack. Before he had a chance to speak, she quickly related what she heard.

"What? Seriously?"

"Yes," she said. "Not only were all four women contestants last year in the annual tropical fruit growing contest at the local fair," she said in exasperation, "but all four are dead. And Marsha said that growing the kiwis is the reason that she's become more alive again after losing her husband ten years ago."

"Well, I guess if anything'll help that, growing something might," he said doubtfully, as if not understanding the attraction for kiwis at all.

"But he didn't die," she said. "When I asked her, she said he just disappeared one day to the next."

Silence.

"Don't you think that's suspicious because Rosie's husband did the same thing ten years ago?"

"Maybe," he said slowly. "But remember, in evidence, none are assumptions."

"We must have assumptions," she argued, "in order to get the evidence."

"Yes, and no," he said.

"Why did you call anyway?" she asked, not wanting to argue right now.

"Mostly because we just found out that Rosie's husband might be alive."

"Of course he is," she said. "Maybe you'll find out that this Marsha woman's husband is alive too."

He snorted. "Not likely," he said. "Lightning rarely strikes in the same place twice."

"No," she said. "Yet we have four little gray-haired ladies all dead with seemingly heart attacks from one moment to the next. And what are the odds of all of them having entered this same contest? It's not that I would expect them to never enter any contest," she said, waving her hand around as she and her animals crossed the street, caught up in her conversation with Mack. "But just think about it. That same contest."

"Do you really think Marsha killed them all to make sure she was the clear-cut winner?"

"No. She seemed clearly surprised to hear of Rosie's death." Doreen thought about the way the woman had smiled over the mention of her kiwis. "I don't think that at all. I don't know what to think," she said in dismay. "But, if one had entered the pie-making contest, and one was in the jam contest, and one was in the celery-growing contest or some godforsaken thing, you would still pick up the fact that all four were big fans of the local fair. But the fact that they were all part of the kiwi-growing contest is just plain weird. I'm not even sure kiwi is growable in Kelowna," she added after a moment.

"I hear you," he said. "Maybe do some research on that for me."

"I can do that," she said, smiling, because most of the time Mack told her to disappear and to not find research forums.

"Have you ever grown any kiwis?"

"No," she said. "I haven't done any vegetable or fruit growing. I was thinking that it would be fun."

"I think it would be," he said. "And that you could eat it too."

She brightened at that. "Funny. I mean, when I was talking about growing vegetables, I wasn't making the connection about eating them. But having food available? That's huge."

"It is," he said. "If nothing else, you could plant at least some salad greens."

"I'd have to see where I could put something," she said, picking up the pace so that she could get home faster. "But I really like that idea. I don't know how expensive seeds are though."

"Seeds are cheap. I might have some hanging around at Mom's place," he said. "She'll never use them."

"Well, it's only Tuesday. I could ask when I go over on Friday," she said.

"Do that," he said. "Spinach and lettuce are easy, and so are radishes. You can always do a pot of chives too."

She grinned. "You know what? I don't know why I never even thought of a vegetable garden," she said. "I spent a lot of my time growing perennials and annuals and making sure the garden was perfect, but I never grew anything that we could eat."

"Well, now you have something else to do. And maybe that's exactly what you need," he said, "something else to keep your mind off the problems in your world."

"I don't have any problems," she said. "As a matter of fact, right now my world is pretty well perfect. You should see the deck and the concrete now. I still have all that gravel to move, and that'll be a real pain, but I was trying to figure out if I needed to put something underneath it first."

"Not if it'll be right along the edge of the concrete," he said. "You may want to dig it back a little bit deeper to stop any of the weeds coming through. I think they say about six inches, but I can give you a hand with that, if you want to wait until the weekend."

"I'll see," she said. "You've done so much for me already. I don't even know how I can thank you."

"How about by butting out of my cases," he said.

"Anything but that," she said cheerfully. "But I will do some research into the kiwis. I just think a whole lot more is going on here that needs to come to light before we solve this."

"And we need the DNA and toxicology report," he said.

"When will that be?"

"Probably Friday," he said. "We're running pretty extensive tests to make sure that we don't leave any rock unturned on this. Like you said, if it were just one or two deaths, then that would have gone unnoticed. But to have had four now ..."

"I am a little worried," she said, "because this Marsha could easily be the next one."

"Maybe," he said in a noncommittal voice.

"I know Nan will be devastated," she said, "if any more of her friends pass on."

"Of course," he said. "And no way to stop it yet."

"I guess an awful lot of little gray-haired ladies are in town, aren't there?" she asked. "So no way to put a protection detail on all them." At his gasp through the phone, she groaned. "Okay, so that was probably a silly statement. I just wish there was a way to protect them."

"Well, they need to not walk off on their own all alone," he said.

"That's another thing," she said. "They were alone, weren't they?"

"Yes." His voice sharpened as he asked, "Why?"

"Just because it's not that common," she said. "Yes, Nan does walk up to see me alone, but I don't think there would be all that many people going out alone at that age. Aren't they afraid of falling or something?" Was that too stereotypical? Because she couldn't imagine anybody telling Marsha that she couldn't go out shopping on her own. "Never mind," she said. "I just realized how foolish that was."

"It's not so foolish," he said, "because I think a lot of people do keep this in mind when they go out for a walk. But one of them was in a parking lot. Remember?"

"Right. So that could have been anybody."

"Exactly. Let's just keep an open mind and keep the assumptions down and the evidence up."

"Yes, I know," she said. "Still, we need to explore all possibilities."

"No," he said. "We need to, not you. You do the research in the kiwis and figure out what you still have time to plant in the garden to see if you can get some homegrown greens in before the winter comes. Other than that, remember that it's time to leave it to the police."

"As long as there are no more murders," she said.

"We don't know that there have been *any* murders," he said, reminding her sharply. "Remember? We need proof, and we need evidence. No assumptions here."

"Fine, but you better hurry up," she said. "I don't want to hear of any more gray-haired ladies dying off on their own."

And this time, she hung up on him. And it made her smile.

Chapter 24

Wednesday Morning...

IT WAS THE next day before Doreen sat down to do some serious research on growing kiwis. She found that, although a lot of people below the forty-ninth parallel had much better success, some people in the Lower Mainland grew kiwis in their backyards but nothing on a commercial level. If they could do it in the Lower Mainland, then, under the right conditions, Kelowna would be a potential gardening mecca for kiwis as well. But again, only on the homegrown varieties and not on a commercial level because the weather was too unstable here.

Down in the Lower Mainland, you could pretty well guarantee that, although it might hit zero degrees or ten below during wintertime, you weren't likely to get the winter temperatures Kelowna would get. And also the Lower Mainland was much less known for extreme heat. So Vancouver would definitely work. She was curious about trying kiwis herself but figured that would take her down a rabbit hole that she didn't dare go. And, if Marsha had any idea that somebody else would appear as an up-and-coming competitor, that might make her much less open to talking to Doreen.

And talking was definitely something Marsha still needed to do. With her name in the Google search bar, Doreen quickly checked out any news that she could find. And, of course, just award after award was mentioned but very little about Marsha's husband. Doreen hadn't even asked what her husband's name was, but Nan might know.

She quickly sent Nan a text, asking her about it.

Nan called instead of texting. In a cross voice, she said, "I don't know everybody in town."

Doreen chuckled. "What did I interrupt you from?" She asked because she knew that Nan never got cross unless she was busy.

"We're lining up the bets," she said. "The cook in the kitchen has a new relationship."

"Oh, gosh, Nan," Doreen groaned. "Do you really bet on people's love lives?"

"Of course," she said. "They're such fun. They can go either way. Nobody really knows anything about it. One moment you think a couple is guaranteed to get together and to stay together, but the next, *poof*, you find out that she ran off with a delivery person or some such thing. Besides, I got these bets covered." And such a note of complacency was in her voice that Doreen had to laugh.

"So, back to my question," Doreen said. "Yes, I know you don't know everybody in town, but I wondered if you knew Marsha and if you knew the name of her husband."

"Ex-husband is what I heard," Nan said. "I think he took off with a younger woman."

"Well, that's a fairly common trait," Doreen said with a wince, thinking about her own husband.

"Sure is," Nan said. "That's why I got rid of the men

before they got older. I figured I might as well be the woman who got rid of them instead of the other way around." And she laughed and laughed.

Doreen smiled. By now, Nan's single life was quite risqué and a bit legendary in Doreen's mind. She didn't have a clue how much of it was even true, but it was fun to think about. "So, does that mean you know, or you don't know?"

"Not sure I do, you know," she said. Her voice turned muffled, as if she had put a hand over the phone. But Doreen could hear her calling to Richie. The discussion went on with Doreen only partially hearing it. "Curtis Langford," Nan said. "We think it's Curtis."

"Okay," Doreen said. "How is Richie doing?"

"Now that you're on the case of Rosie's will," Nan said with a happy tone, "he's much better."

"Rosie was well-liked, wasn't she?"

"Absolutely," Nan said. "The others were too. Although I didn't know two of them very well."

"Rosie was on her way up to my house," Doreen said, knowing that she was walking a minefield here if she put it the wrong way. "Any idea if the other three women would have gone shopping or walking alone?" She could almost hear Nan bristling over the phone. "I'm just asking if that was their customary habit," Doreen said quietly. "Not that they weren't capable or needed to be chauffeured around or had to be escorted. I'm looking at what their daily habits were."

"No clue. Rosie didn't go out alone very often," Nan said grudgingly. "She often took somebody with her for a walk. But, of course, we know why she didn't this time."

"Maybe, but she could have come with you," Doreen said.

"Maybe," she said, "but she didn't even tell me that she was going to see you." And, for that, Nan grumped a little louder as she added, "Don't know why."

"Maybe because she wanted to keep it a secret about what she was doing."

"Well, I can keep secrets," Nan said.

"You're very good at keeping secrets," Doreen agreed. "I was just checking."

"You'd have to ask some of the family members."

"Yeah, that's part of my list today," Doreen said with a nod.

After she hung up, she realized that's exactly what she needed to do—find out more about these older women's daily habits. With their names written down, she wondered if she could intrude a little bit upon the family members or if it would be too much, too soon. She frowned as she thought about it and then called the first one and got an elderly daughter of Bella Beauty. When Doreen explained who she was, the woman appeared thrilled. "Oh my," she said. "I've seen you walking around town. I do love that bird on your shoulder."

Almost as if knowing he was being charmed, Thaddeus walked to the phone and said, "Thaddeus is here. Thaddeus is here."

The other woman laughed and laughed. "Oh my," she said. "I needed that today. We buried Mom a few days ago and it's been a little hard."

"And I'm so sorry about that," Doreen said sadly. "It's hard when we lose those we love."

"Exactly," she said. "And it was such a strange thing."

"What was strange?" Doreen asked.

"Well, she wanted to go for a walk alone," she said. "She

was acting secretive about it."

"She didn't go with anybody?"

"Not that I know of. I was at work. I'm almost done," she said. "Another few months and I would retire and spend the last few years with Mom. And now I feel like I should keep working so I have something to do."

"Don't make a decision too quickly," Doreen said, as she stared into the phone. "You'll have enough tough days early on that you'll go from one answer to another. Give yourself a little bit of time to see a future without your mother first."

"Yes, those are very good words of wisdom," the daughter said. "But, no, I don't think she was going with anybody. But I don't know. Maybe she was meeting somebody."

"Was she active in the gardening fair at all?"

"Oh, yes," she said. "As a matter of fact, several of us are doing a newsletter about a couple friends who passed away within weeks of each other. We're pretty sure they were just so heartsick about losing their friends. Mom was the first, of course, and, although I half expected her to go anytime, I didn't really expect it. ... You never do until it actually happens."

"True enough," Doreen said. "I think that goes for any major change in life."

"Quite true," the woman said. "Anyway, we'll do a celebration of her life and talk about her gardening and her friends and how close they were all these years."

"So the three of them who had passed away here recently were all good friends?"

"Oh, yes," she said. "They were the best of friends."

"Oh my," Doreen said. "That's both sad and lovely."

"Right?"

"And they were all involved in gardening, weren't they?"

"They were," she said. "But I think my mom was much more interested in the kiwi part of it. The others were more than happy to go along with it though."

"Why kiwis?"

"Oh, that answer is easy. It was Marsha," she said. "All they wanted to do was upset Marsha so she wasn't the champion any longer."

"That's an odd reason for growing kiwis though," Doreen said with a laugh.

"Well, Marsha used to be part of the same gang," she said. "And then everybody kept putting in for various contests. And some of them got blue ribbons, and some of them got top mentions and things like that, but nobody ever really locked into a niche area that they won over and over again. Except for Marsha."

"And did that grate on the others?"

"Over time it did, yes," Bella's daughter said. "I wish, if I could have given my mother one thing, it was a chance to win that contest."

"So they grew kiwis so they had something valuable or something that was viable as a contest entry?"

"They were trying to do anything that would make them a winner," she said. "It was just friendly rivalry, but, after Marsha found her niche, it was hard for the others to not find something for themselves. So they started to compete against her. And again, it all started in good fun, but, over the last few years, it hasn't been much fun."

"Understandable," Doreen said. "My own grandmother can get fairly fanatical about certain things."

"Right? Anyway," the daughter said, "she's at rest now."

"I understand," she said. "I was looking into all the different deaths, and I heard about the kiwi connection and thought I'd call and ask. I didn't mean to intrude."

"Not intruding at all," the daughter said. "I love to talk about Mom. We were very close, and she'll be sadly missed." At that, the daughter started to sniffle.

Doreen hurriedly said, "Thank you very much for speaking with me then." And she hung up.

She got up and walked around the house, trying to deal with her own sense of loss because it brought up the reminder that Nan wasn't as young as she used to be, and her death could happen any time too. Whether natural or unnatural, that was scary to think about. Obviously it was worse to consider somebody had helped these old ladies to their deaths. But to consider that four were struck down by Mother Nature just like that?

Well, it's not something Doreen wanted to consider. She had visions of Nan being one hundred years old and driving her cronies wacky with her betting. The odds weren't necessarily in her favor, but she was in good health, so she'd go as long as she could go. As long as Doreen could make sure that nobody would help her nan into the grave, like maybe these other women had been *helped*. And it was interesting to consider that all these dead women had been friends with Marsha, until now one of them had risen above within the kiwi-growing community.

Doreen couldn't get her mind wrapped around the kiwis. They were harder to grow than avocados for sure, and certainly bananas were a nonstarter here, and citrus had to be greenhoused and cared for gently. But it was possible to grow lemons and oranges in Kelowna. It's just that they had to be mothered all the time. Doreen wasn't sure if she was up for that kind of gardening, but it did spike her interest. She was particularly wondering about fruit trees. Just little ones that she could keep pruned, and anything food-related was a good idea as far as she was concerned, and that had her up and walking outside to her new deck to view her garden.

Every time she came out here, she wanted to dance and sing in joy. She skipped down the few steps onto the sidewalk and laughed. "Look at this, Mugs. Just look at this," she said. And she raced down to the creek and back to the deck again. Mugs barked and danced around her, matching her step for step. Thaddeus flew partway, landed, picked up, flew a little bit, and then got sidetracked by something in the grass. He started pecking away, while Doreen laughed.

Goliath, on the other hand, stretched out in the sun along the top step on the deck and dropped his head and rolled onto his back, leaving his big furry tummy open for the fresh breeze. She reached down and gave him a bit of a belly scratch. He didn't even move. "I'm glad to see you guys all approve," she said.

It was stupendous. She walked to the two spots where the men had left her room for a garden, right where the railings were. It was definitely big enough to put something in. She just didn't know what. Something bright and cheerful would be nice to help counteract all the wood. As much as she loved wood, it could use a little bit of a change in color and tone.

Finally she stopped her dancing and jumping about, gasping for air, but having enjoyed the racing back and forth, and just stood and marveled at her backyard. She did have room for a few small trees and definitely could put some vegetable gardens in. Mack was right. It would be lovely to have some fresh salad, homegrown by her. She was such a rabbit, so why hadn't she even considered rabbit food? Because a vegetable planting was so far from her realm of experience, and yet she was a gardener. She thrived on it. So how did she end up with this big blank spot in her world?

He had mentioned something about seeds and how they weren't expensive and, if she went online, she could probably find a bunch. It might be too late to find any seeds to buy in a local gardening center. Were there any still open? She frowned as she thought about it. It was late June already; still there should be time for sowing at least lettuce and maybe green onions, potentially some of the faster-growing vegetables. She'd have to do some research and figure it out.

As she headed back inside to her kitchen, her mind wandered back to the four dead women. One had been walking in a parking lot alone, and that didn't seem all that strange. Another one had gone for a walk on her own, and one had been found on the sidewalk alone, and one had been in a park. All four of those weren't odd in their own right. But one had seemed secretive and maybe was meeting somebody. Doreen wondered who and why.

She quickly dialed the son of the second woman, Kimmy Schwartz, knowing that men were much less prone to talk about things, like what Bella's daughter had been very focused on.

"And what do you want?" he snapped at her when he learned who she was.

She winced at that. "I was just speaking with the daughter of Bella Beauty," she explained carefully. "There was talk about doing a newsletter to celebrate the women's lives."

His tone mollified somewhat, he said, "That'll be something my wife will handle. My mother was a sweet old lady, and it was her time. That's all there was to it."

"Did she often go walking outside alone like that?"

"No," he said. "She said she was meeting somebody, an

old friend. Somebody she was trying to heal a rift with, and I don't know if she did or not, but I would hope so because it's important to her in her soul that she's cleared as many of her debts as she possibly could."

At his tone of voice, Doreen winced slightly. "I hope so too, for her sake. Thank you very much for talking with me."

At that, he hung up without even saying goodbye. She tried to dial one of the family members of the other woman, Delilah, but there was no answer. Doreen would have to try them later.

Now for the fourth woman. Rosie's family and that'll be Danny. That wasn't so good. She quickly sent Mack a text regarding Delilah's family. He sent back a question. **Why?**

Wanted to contact him or her about the club they had formed to usurp Marsha as the kiwi-growing queen, she replied.

When her phone rang again, she laughed into it.

"Are you serious?"

"Yes," she said and quickly told Mack what Bella's daughter had shared.

"You weren't thinking Marsha killed them, are you?"

"Oh, that's an interesting thought," she said. "I don't know that that would be too extreme, considering what we know about murderers."

"But still, you don't just win a competition like that by killing the competition."

"That's exactly what you do," Doreen said, laughing. "Because then nobody has a viable chance against you."

"I can't imagine it," he said.

"Well, if you find the two missing husbands, you could ask them. Maybe they had something to do with it too."

"Well, I'm still working on that," he said.

"You know what? Come to think of it, I'm not sure either of the other two had husbands," she said quietly. "Do you know?"

"Both are deceased," he said grudgingly.

"So, we have four single old ladies, widowed, interested in gardening, and interested in the kiwi competition, all dropped dead, leaving only one queen in the kiwi competition, and her husband is missing."

"And you're thinking it's all connected?" A note of humor and curiosity melded together in his voice.

"How can it not be?" she said. "They know each other, and they're in the same competition every year. They used to be friends but are no longer friends."

"What about the grandson?" he asked. "You thought he might be responsible."

"Well, I wouldn't put it past him," she said. "Maybe he was trying to curry favor by killing off the other people in the contest." Mack snorted at that. "Just look at him," she said. "He's kind of sleazy."

"Well, that sleaze has been cleared too, by the way."

"That's too bad," she said with heartfelt frustration. "He's not exactly the upstanding citizen we want to have around."

"It doesn't matter if you want it or not," he said. "We didn't have a reason to consider him any longer."

"He attacked Richie and me," she said.

"Maybe, but you didn't want to press charges either."

"What about the letter to me? Did you find any fingerprints?"

"Only hers."

"The will? Any luck with that yet?"

"It appears to be the most recent and legal, yes," he said.

"What about the people who witnessed it?" she asked. "Did you prove without any shred of doubt that the manor had something to do with this, had coerced Rosie into signing that version of the will?"

"I don't believe so," he said. "One of them signed it on her last day. Apparently she was really good friends with Rosie and had been happy to do that. And she'd hated the grandson too. Nobody at the place liked him, as he constantly came in and left Rosie in tears."

"And that's not very nice," Doreen said. "I couldn't imagine going to Nan's place and leaving her upset."

"No," he said, "but you're a very different kind of fish."

"Did you figure out why the grandson needed money so badly?"

"He's about to lose his house," Mack said comfortably. "He's a big spender and likes to impress the girlfriends. Taken four weekends down to the coast and off to the island, even Seattle up to Banff, and charging it all on his credit card. Now he's unable to pay it back, so he took out a second mortgage on his house to pay off his creditors, but now he can't pay his double payments on the house."

"Wow," she said. "He must really have no idea how money works to do something like that."

"I think it was more of how he didn't understand how women work," Mack said in a dry tone.

"Good point," she said with a chuckle. "Fine. If he didn't have anything to do with her death then, whatever, but I'm still a little worried about that. Has he been told what's in the will?"

"Don't know yet," Mack said. "I haven't talked to the lawyer today."

"Interesting," she said. "Rosie didn't have much, but I'm

sure the grandson will be devastated if he doesn't get anything."

"According to the witness who signed her will, I spoke with her this morning," he said, "the grandson knew that his grandmother was planning on doing this. She'd threatened it many times."

"But I wonder, when you threaten something like that, when push comes to shove," Doreen said, "if you actually go through with it. He is her only flesh and blood. Unless, of course, her husband is still alive."

"True enough," Mack said. "And we still haven't located the missing husbands—Rosie's or Marsha's."

"Right," she said. "I feel like that's connected too."

"In what way?"

"I don't know," she said. "I did get Marsha's husband's name, it is Curtis Langford, but I haven't done any research on him yet."

In the background, she could hear Mack typing away. "We don't have any report here of a missing person named Curtis Langford."

"So that would mean that she never went to the cops about it, right?"

"Yes," he said.

"Nan suggested that he ran away with a younger woman," she said, "so we could check her marital status and see if she got divorced."

"Their last names are the same. Plus he might not have divorced her," Mack warned. "Why would he just because he found somebody younger to go play with for a while? It doesn't mean he wanted to go through a legal divorce."

"No," she said. "There is the house, and it's quite lovely, so he must have money of his own for him to live off of and must have left her well enough off that she wouldn't complain."

"Good point," Mack said. "And what would that take, I wonder."

"I don't know," she said. "When you think about it, most women want revenge or to get something for being left behind."

"Like you?"

"I'm the opposite, apparently," she said. "I didn't want to have anything to do with him."

"Well, we'll see what my brother says this weekend."

Chapter 25

Wednesday Early Afternoon ...

DOREEN COULDN'T LET go of the missing husbands coincidence. It seemed to be an interesting added fact that connected four of these women. Or at least two of them. Two dead husbands, two missing husbands. Was it that common for husbands to go missing? She assumed that, in some cases, it meant he had run off with a younger woman, but it made her feel odd to consider it.

In her case, she had been the one who had left and not necessarily by choice either. She'd been pinched out. If she'd known that her husband had been running off with another woman too, Doreen would have taken off a long time ago. But her husband wouldn't let her go then either. She frowned as she considered the truth of that matter. He'd been very controlling, and everything happened in his time frame. And, for the first time, she was wondering, looking at meeting Mack's brother this weekend with a little bit more joy. It's not that she wanted to get back at her husband, but she wanted to have her life free and clear.

A yawn caught her by surprise. It was already early afternoon, and she hadn't done anything. She had lazed the day away. The walk had helped, but even now she was sitting here doing nothing. And that was mostly because it had been such a rough weekend with people upon people around.

The result of all those people's work had been absolutely stunning, but it didn't change the fact that she had a lot of work still to do. And that she'd have to do it herself, like moving some of that gravel. Calling the animals to her, she stepped into her backyard, found the wheelbarrow, grabbed her gardening gloves, and moved out to the front. She slowly filled the wheelbarrow with gravel to the point where she could still push it and moved it to the backyard.

As she did so, her mind was buzzing on the vegetable gardening and on the missing husbands. It didn't make any sense. It would help if she had an image of them. Maybe that would assist her to sort out where these men had disappeared to. She couldn't pinpoint why it was important to the case. Just that another thread dangled, and she didn't like dangling threads. She wanted her *T*s crossed and her *I*s dotted. Who knew she would be such a stickler for details? But every untied thread like this just left open for interpretation what really happened—and even the tiniest answer could make a major difference to the actual mystery.

When she got the wheelbarrow around to the backyard, she stopped and studied where it should go and decided the easiest was to start way down at the farthest end of the sidewalk. The creek was already trickling upward, as the water rose in the evening, then dropped again in the morning, so that some of the edges on the path alongside the creek were filling with water. She grabbed her edger, cutting the grass back along her sidewalks, so she had about four inches cut away from the concrete and four inches deep, and then slowly shoveled the new trench full of gravel. That should give her enough of a good crisp and deep edge to put in the gravel.

The wheelbarrow load of gravel went a lot farther than she thought too. With that emptied, she went and refilled it, then came back with the edger and her shovel and worked on another deep trench all along the side until she could fill it up again with gravel. By the time she'd done one side, she stood, admiring the look. "What do you think, Mugs?"

He walked along the edge, sticking his paws into the gravel and shifting it around underneath his paw. He immediately switched over to the grass and walked on it instead. "I get you," she said, "but this is interesting. I like the look of that." She filled the wheelbarrow up again and again, until she had done all the edges of the concrete leading from the creek up to the patio, and then she had to decide what to do on both sides of the house. When she filled the wheelbarrow the next time, she filled in some of the missing places along the driveway to the back, up to and along the house. Then she did the same on the far side. She had a little bit of gravel left, but it was not a ton. She looked at it and realized that pretty well, to keep the same look, she needed to do an edge of gravel around the outside of the patio too. That would take a little more cutting work though.

With her nifty edger, she went to work on another big trench all the way around her patio. It took longer than she thought, but most of that was because the shoveling itself was also that much slower for her. By the time she'd done the left side of the patio, she only had one side remaining and another three estimated wheelbarrow loads of gravel available. She stopped and wiped her forehead. "You know what? We'll need dinner after this. Won't we, guys?"

Mugs woofed, but he was lying on his back and trying to

scratch his head in the grass, his feet skyward. He was enjoying a chance to be outside playing.

She managed to get the last part of the patio edged all the way around to where the patio joined the sidewalk to go around the house, and she tied it up nice and neat. She had a little bit of gravel left, so she loaded it up in her empty wheelbarrow, and she walked along, adding a bit to wherever it looked like it still needed a little more. But it looked amazing by the time she was done.

With the last of her energy, she scooped up all the bits and pieces that she had cut out and loaded it all up into the wheelbarrow and with that, she took it out to the front, using her sidewalk every step of the way and then piled it all into the compost bin. Done, she moved the wheelbarrow back and grabbed the broom from her garage, then quickly swept the driveway from where the gravel had been. She moved it all off to the side and just like that, another job was done.

Smiling, she headed back inside and tried to figure out what she would eat. A sandwich didn't appeal, and an omelet would be more substantial, but she really wanted meat. Yet the ham she had didn't entice her. She had no more pizza leftovers, so it would be a big chef's salad maybe or an omelet after all. She frowned at that though because she was a bit chilled from being so tired after all that hard work in her backyard and decided to make a heftier omelet.

With her eggs in the pan, she quickly laid quite a bit of ham on top of it and then cheese and a few mushrooms. By the time the omelet was cooked, it was bigger than anything she'd made yet. She put it on the plate and smiled. "If you could only see me now, Mack," she whispered. But he probably would have said she could have done a whole lot different than this. She took the first bite and sat back, hearing her stomach grumble as it was being teased. She smiled and whispered to Mugs, "This is wonderful."

He jumped up onto his back legs, putting his front legs onto her thigh, and sniffed her plate. She chuckled. "You'll have to wait until I'm done," she said. "I'm a little too hungry right now."

Indeed, she didn't slow down until she got to the last quarter. There, she stopped and pushed her plate back a little bit. "So maybe my eyes were bigger than my tummy," she said. "But then I did do five eggs."

She rolled her eyes at that because she was sure her husband would have had a fit. He believed that eggs would cause her cholesterol to rise and fat to form on her thighs. But then he'd been very, very worried about her thighs and her hips and her waistline. She slowly had another bite and ate it, and, by the time she was down to the last bite, she cut it up into little pieces and put it on the floor for Mugs. He devoured the entire thing without even thinking about it.

She got up, put on the teakettle, and rinsed her fry pan and flipper. When Mugs was done, she washed her plate, knife, and fork, and then she quickly fed all the animals. She still had some fruit in her fridge, so she grabbed an apple and took her pot of tea outside to the new patio. With a beautiful deck now, she wasn't sure she should sit on the patio or up on the deck. She didn't have furniture for both. And the patio had been easier originally, but now she really wasn't sure.

With her cup of tea, she walked over and sat on the steps and sighed happily. The sidewalk stretched down toward the creek in front of her, and she could see all her hard work from today as well. She grabbed her laptop and brought it out to sit on her lap while she leaned up against the railing. It was perfect. She could sit all over the place. And still work too.

She brought up pictures of Curtis, Marsha's husband, and noted his features. A couple photos of him were from various prominent volunteer positions he'd held. A big affable man with a rounded chest and always had his arm hooked around Marsha's shoulders. They looked happy together. It didn't look like he'd be the kind to run off with a younger woman at all. Frowning, she kept looking through more, going farther back into Google's archives. Sometimes his name brought up hundreds of pages, and it took time to sort through them.

When she finally took a look for Rosie's husband, David McDougal, she found much less in the way of pictures. It was mostly Rosie's photos and not David's. And then she found one with his hat on and his face turned to the side. She frowned at that. She picked up her phone and called Nan. "Hey, Nan. I know you said earlier how Rosie's husband was a layabout, with his gambling and his supposed gardening. But what did Rosie's husband do to earn a living?"

"He was a salesman," she said. "Medical supply company or something like that. Why?"

"Just, you know, if he took off on her …"

"I don't know that he did that though," Nan said. "I don't really see it as being something he would do."

"The women were all friends, right?"

"The other three women were friends with Marsha," Nan said. "Yes. But not Rosie."

"She wasn't friends with Marsha?"

"No, no, not like the others were. They were the kiwi

clique. Carried those stupid things around everywhere. Rosie, instead of arguing with them, used to hand them out to everyone instead. Especially to the four of them. Almost as a reminder that she was there and would usurp the reigning Kiwi Queen."

Ahhh, bingo. "But Rosie wasn't having trouble with any of them, was she?"

"Only Marsha," she said. "And that was over the kiwi contest. She knew the other ladies and was friendly to them, but it wasn't the same thing. The other three were *friends* friends."

Chapter 26

Wednesday Midafternoon ...

AFTER THE CALL, Doreen struggled to understand the relationship between the women. But she felt the missing men was where the key lay. Something about friendly women with dead husbands. The fact that there had never been any reports on either of them also concerned her. Did the men get up and walk away? And nobody cared? Or did they send back notices, saying, *Don't let the police know where I've gone or don't bother calling the police because I'm still alive, but you're never getting a divorce*? She didn't understand that mentality. But then, she hadn't done anything about her divorce or fixing the problems she had either, so maybe it was the same kind of disowning or trying to disavow the issues. She sat here for a long time, studying the men, when she called Nan again. "Do you know anybody who knew her husband?"

"Which husband?"

"Rosie's husband," she said.

"Not really," she said. "Why?"

"I wanted to know if he would have had an affair with any of the other women in that group," Doreen asked.

Nan sucked in her breath. "Now that you mention it ..." And her voice trailed off.

"He did, didn't he?"

"Rosie's husband had a bit of a wandering eye," Nan admitted. "He propositioned me more than a time or two."

Doreen closed her eyes and winced. "Please tell me that you didn't take him up on it."

"Of course not," Nan said stoutly. "Who do you think I am? I only dated men who were completely available. And Rosie was my friend. I'd never do that to her."

"Good," Doreen said. And she meant it because, as much as she would love and forgive Nan for it, she felt that Nan would be a much better person to have not crossed that line. And that she would go do her own thing and make her a happier soul. And that brought back the words of Kimmy Schwartz's son, about healing old rifts, setting things right. "Any idea who he might have had an affair with?"

"I think it was Marsha," she said. "I think that's what was between the two of them." She stopped for a moment, paused, and said, "Or was it the other way around?"

"Marsha's husband and Rosie?"

"Yeah," Nan said slowly. "Of course, that's what the gossip mill says. Rosie had never mentioned anything to me though."

"How long have you known her?"

"Twenty-plus years," Nan said eerily. "But we didn't always see each other all that time. You know? Like a lot of friends, you see each other, and then you don't see or talk to them for six months, and then you meet them in a coffee shop, sit down, catch up, and carry on again. We've really only managed to spend some consecutive time together once we were both here, and I've only been here for about four

months maybe. Sometime before you moved in the house."
She laughed. "I should have moved in years ago."

Doreen smiled. "And I should have left years ago too,"
she admitted. "But we're both happy to be where we are
right now."

"Happy is a mild word for it," Nan said. "I never knew
all these old people could be so interesting, if for no other
reason than their curiosities—their foibles, their little
argumentative things, the stuff that they must get just right. I
always knew I was pretty easygoing, but I didn't really see it
until I got here."

Doreen's eyes widened at that. "You also have a chance
to do things that you never really spent much time on, like
lawn bowling."

"True, true, true," she said. "Not to mention so many
more opportunities for gambling. It's such a lovely hobby."

"Says you," Doreen said, wincing.

"It's been good for me here," Nan said. "I hated to admit it to myself, but I was lonely sometimes living in that
house all alone."

"Well, you aren't alone anymore," Doreen said with a
smile. "I'm here to spend time with you."

"Why don't you come for a cup of tea then?" Nan asked.
"It's been kind of a black morning. Everybody's down about
Rosie. They're all making memorial plans, and it's getting
everybody depressed."

"I'd love to come. I'm sitting out on my brand-new
deck," she said with a laugh. "Trying to do some research
into Marsha and Rosie, and that's why I was wondering
about the husbands."

"Well, you come on down," Nan said, "and I'll hop
across and talk to Midge, see if she's home. She might know

something too." With that, Nan hung up.

Doreen put her laptop inside, set the security, and thought of the jewels. She still had to deal with them when a new appraiser came to town. When she got that appraisal back, then she could set up a price and determine how to divide the rest of it. But she had yet to talk to Mack about that. Tossing all that old stuff to the back of her mind, she was much happier to deal with the current mystery.

With her animals in tow, she walked along the creek, noticing that this time the pathway was wet, as if the water had risen in the night to cover up the path and had receded enough during the day to reveal it again. She could still walk the path, and it was a little on the slippery side, but it meant that maybe in the next day or two she couldn't walk along here at all. She made her way around the corner and down toward Nan's with a bright smile. She saw Nan sitting outside, waiting for her. The animals raced ahead.

As she got there, Nan looked up from cuddling Mugs and Goliath and smiled. "I managed to walk into the dining room and grab us cream puffs," she said. "I hit up Midge afterward, but she didn't know anything more than I did." She somehow managed to impart that information with a self-satisfied sniff. As if happy to know Midge didn't have more gossip than Nan did.

"Cream puffs?" Doreen asked with a big smile. "I don't even think I've had any in decades."

"Well, you're in for a treat then," she said. "I also scooped up a bit of cream for the animals."

Doreen laughed as she walked along the flagstones. It was hard to remember that Fred wasn't here anymore. "Any news about Frank and Fred? Did you guys hire a new gardener?"

"Fred's out on bail," she said. "The management here had a meeting about it, and they decided that he was innocent until proven guilty, so he will be back working again."

Doreen smiled and nodded. "I'm quite happy to hear that," she said. "I didn't really want to see him suffer."

"Oh, I think that family's had plenty of suffering," Nan said with a dark overtone.

"Which is why I didn't want him to have more," she said. As she sat down, she studied the plate in front of her with the lovely little buns with cream in the center and little hats of cream too. "These look lovely," she said.

"Absolutely. I love these. Pick one," Nan urged.

"It's hard to pick one," Doreen murmured. "They look so pretty."

Nan chuckled, reached over to the plate, picked up one, and put it on her plate. "I got two for each of us," she said. "I'm not sure if I'll eat both of mine though." And she picked it up and took a bite. Immediately whipping cream gushed out on both sides, and she had dusted her nose with icing sugar. Nan laughed and said, "They're delicious."

Doreen picked one up, wondering how she was supposed to eat something like that. But, given Nan's enthusiasm and lack of care, she followed suit. She did a better job of it but still ended up with cream coming out everywhere. She shook her head. "Is there an easy way to eat these?"

"Nope," Nan said, as she continued to munch through hers. "Just eat them because they're so good."

Doreen followed suit and finished licking the rest of the cream off her fingers. She had a big dollop on her plate too. She picked that up and let Mugs lick it off her finger and then grabbed another little bit for Thaddeus. He sat here, staring at it. As Goliath hopped up unto her lap and looked at her plate and then up at her, she took a little bit of cream off the top of the second cream puff and gave it to him. "They don't need the sugar," she said, "but apparently the cream is going down just lovely."

"Of course it is," Nan says. "Everybody needs a treat."

"Maybe," Doreen said with a smile. "I'm not sure I need the sugar though."

"Don't go on about your weight again," Nan said. "Unless it's to say you're trying to gain weight."

Doreen chuckled. "I'm doing much better," she said. "With Mack feeding me all the time, that's working out lovely."

"Yes, but are you learning anything?" Nan asked.

"A little," she said. "I'm getting quite proficient with omelets. But I definitely need to open my repertoire."

"Good," Nan said. "How about pasta?"

"I've cooked plain noodles," Doreen admitted. "But only with Mack there to watch."

Nan chuckled and reached over for a second cream puff. "I don't need it," she said, "but I'll have it." This time she opened it, so there was cream on both halves and slowly ate each half.

Doreen looked at it, nodded, and said, "That looks much less messy." So she cut her second one in half too.

"But it doesn't taste nearly as good," Nan said with a laugh.

"I did it this way, thinking I might not eat the whole thing," Doreen explained.

"In your case," Nan stated, "you can eat the whole thing."

But Doreen still preferred it cut open and worked her way slowly through the second one. When she put down the second half and picked up her tea to have a sip, she murmured, "That's a good cup of tea, Nan."

"This is a blend of herbs I made for Rosie all the time," Nan said sadly. "She'll be missed."

"I'm sorry," Doreen said. "It's so much harder to lose a friend, isn't it?"

"It is, indeed," Nan said with a sigh.

"I'm hoping that nobody comes after you," Doreen said. "So make sure you don't walk anywhere alone."

"Unless I call you first and you meet me at the creek," she said with a decisive nod. "Besides, the drugs could have been given at any time. They could have had tea together. They could have been administered here at the manor," she said, turning to look around. "It's hard to say."

"I know," Doreen said. "That's why I'm concerned. We don't want it to be something that you could be touched with and have it kill you."

"Rosie used to grow digitalis," she said.

"Right," Doreen said. "Didn't you too?"

"I did for a while," she said. "We know Penny did as well."

"Of course, but it's a matter of making a concoction that's strong enough to get them to ingest it? And to have it affect them later? Unless they were meeting somebody each time."

"Well, Rosie was coming to you, but she might have been talking to somebody else." Nan frowned. "I did hear her voice as she left. She was talking on the phone too."

"To meet someone?" Doreen leaned closer. "Because I know one of the women, Bella Beauty, was to meet someone.

I spoke to her daughter. Bella was to meet somebody. Somebody she was trying to bury the hatchet with."

"So it's hard to say then," Nan said. "But that sounds like something that Rosie would do as well." And then she stopped, looked at Doreen, and said, "It would be something all us older ladies would likely do too because we're always trying to clear off our plates and make amends for anything we might have done wrong."

"But did they do anything wrong?"

"I doubt Rosie did," she said. "But I know it bothered her that Marsha wasn't a friend."

"But why would she be bothered?"

"Exactly," Nan said with a nod. "I'm pretty sure that, somewhere between those two couples, there was a crossover."

"But you don't know which direction?"

"Nope, and I know Rosie was mystified by Marsha's good luck in her growing the kiwis."

"In most cases, it's usually the perfect conditions," Doreen said. "You know? Great nutrition, water, sunshine, away from the breeze ... There could be all kinds of things that made her kiwis outstanding."

"I know," she said. "And Rosie had an idea herself."

"And why did it really matter to her that she beat Marsha?"

"It became more than a competition. It became an ugly competition," she said. "It's the only part of Rosie's personality I didn't like."

"Meaning that she got quite ugly about it?"

"Very competitive. So I don't think she would have met Marsha, unless Marsha was willing to talk to her about the kiwis ..."

"Is there any reason why Marsha would want to meet Rosie?"

"I don't think so," she said.

"Did either of them have any money issues?"

"If anybody did, it would be Rosie," she said. "But she never appeared to really need anything. And Marsha has a big house, so I don't think she's suffering for money."

"I'd love to get into these women's financials," Doreen said.

"That little address book you took away," Nan said, "did you ever get those stuck pages apart?"

"I forgot about it," Doreen said. "I did try to get the pages open when I got home, but something's stuck in there."

"Toss it in the freezer," Nan said. "If it's gum, it'll come off."

"Did she chew gum?"

"All the time," Nan said.

Doreen nodded, remembering quite a bit of gum had been in Rosie's night table. "I can try that when I get home." She sat and visited a little bit longer, trying to get any information she could, but there was really nothing to be had. Finally she got up, took her leave, gathering her animals to head home, coming to where they'd found Rosie's body. That bothered Doreen too. She stopped at the spot, where somebody had put flowers.

It looked like the gladiolas she'd seen at Marsha's house. She stopped and looked at the little card that said, "Stay safe, Rosie."

What an odd thing to say. She took a photo of the card and kept on walking to her house. It was lovely that somebody would put that memorial there, but it did make her question the underlying theme behind it.

She and her animals wandered up the creek. It was a slow walk because it was that much slipperier and would probably be the last time she'd go down this pathway for a while. When she got back home again, she picked up the tiny book that had the pages stuck and realized that it could be gum between the two. She tossed it into the freezer. Then, deciding that she needed to check on Marsha and see if she had left that little card, Doreen headed out for another walk in the opposite direction. Her animals were only too happy to join her, like she had kept them cooped up all day long.

She wished a grocery store was nearby, where she could walk to it and maybe even pick up one of those rotisserie chickens. Sometimes they were on sale really cheap, and that would make a lovely salad and sandwich. Not to mention she could sit at home and just eat chicken.

Chuckling to herself, she walked through the cul-de-sac and headed toward where Heidi and Aretha's house was. As she walked past Aretha's house, she saw no sign of anybody, but she lifted a hand, just in case, and waved, then kept on going. When she got around to Marsha's house, she saw no sign of anybody there. She walked past and called out, "Hello?"

Marsha walked around from the backyard. She frowned at Doreen and said, "Oh, it's you again."

This time, there was no sign of the friendly woman she'd met earlier.

Doreen smiled brightly. "Yes, it's me. Your flowers are still doing so lovely," she said, motioning at the huge gladiolas in front of her. "Do you ever sell them at the market?"

"I don't have time to be bothered with that," Marsha said.

"I just came from the manor, and I thought I saw the same shade that you've got here."

"It's not all that unusual," Marsha said.

"No, maybe not," Doreen said. "Still, it was a lovely gesture on your part."

The woman shrugged uncomfortably. "How would you know the flowers were from me?"

"I don't," Doreen said quietly realizing with this admission Marsha knew what she was talking about. She only said she'd been to the manor before not the spot they found Rosie. "The blooms look very much the same."

"Like I said, it could be plants from anybody," she said. "Lots of them have this same shade."

"I don't know about that," she said. "I know Heidi a few doors away has some, but I'm pretty sure Heidi is still in jail."

"I never would have thought of her being guilty of anything. She has always had the sweetest smile."

"Same with Rosie," Doreen said with a half smile. "Her sweet personality and that lovely smile will be missed." But Doreen's attempt to draw out Marsha a little bit failed. At least the animals were being good for once, maybe even a little serious as if understanding the solemn conversation. "But then I gathered some bad blood was between the two of you, with the affair and all."

Marsha slowly straightened, her eyes glazing over. "What are you talking about?"

Doreen frowned. "I'm sorry. I didn't mean to step on toes," she said. "I just heard that your husband had an affair with her."

At that, Marsha snorted. "You think that would have been the end of it, if it was, wouldn't it? But it wasn't. He didn't have anything to do with that woman," she sneered. "Why would he?"

"Well, I certainly understand when men step out," Doreen said softly, "having experienced the same thing myself."

Marsha's eyebrows shot up. "Seriously?"

Doreen nodded. "Yes."

"Well, it wasn't the same for me," Marsha said, staring off in the distance. "Bloody men though, they can't keep their peckers in their pants, can they?"

"Not all of them, no," Doreen said. "Some of them are good guys. And others, well, they don't have the same ability to resist something that's in front of them, even if it's not offered."

Marsha snorted at that again. "Well, I can see that you think you know what you're talking about," she said, "but you don't. However, I won't be missing Rosie's presence on this planet Earth anytime soon." And, with that, she stormed off.

Confused and yet curious, Doreen meandered back home again. She noted an alleyway at the back of Marsha's house too. She went around the back and studied it, wondering if Marsha was close by too. Or could Doreen walk up and look into Marsha's backyard without being seen?

Doreen walked down the alleyway quietly. She could see Marsha going into the kitchen from the back area and slamming the door shut behind her. Even as Doreen watched, blinds dropped down to stop anybody from looking in. Good enough. That meant that at least then Doreen didn't have to worry about Marsha staring at her.

She walked past, looking around at the neighbors. One old guy was lugging something out to the garbage. She walked over to help him. "You need a hand with that?"

"Sure," he said, huffing a little bit. "The doctors don't want me lifting much over my head, and I've already dragged this sucker down here." It looked to be old and part of a sectional couch.

"Where did you want to put it?" she asked curiously. He pointed to the trailer there beside him. She grabbed an end and tried to drag it. "Wow. It's heavy," she said. She tried again and managed to get it moved a little bit, and he pushed and she pulled, and they got it over to the ramp to aid them. She hopped onto the trailer, and slowly they managed to get it loaded up.

"That was quite a job," she said, squatting and staring at the broken couch.

"And I thank you for your help," he said. "It would have just sat here until I could get somebody to load it for me. And, once the rain comes, it would have turned into a nasty, moldy, and heavier mess than ever." He reached out a hand. "My name is Trumper."

She smiled at that. "Is that a nickname?"

"Sure is," he said. "I was part of a drum cadet band, and I used to roll out the call all the time, so they called me Trumper."

She didn't quite follow, but she laughed. "Hey, I like it," she said. She hopped down off the trailer. "Have you lived out here all your life?"

"I must look like I'm old and half-buried in this place already, huh?"

She grinned. "Nope. I've met a lot of people who have had homes for all their lives here and had never moved."

"Moved here back in the '60s. Found my home, and I stuck here. Been married and widowed twice," he said with a sad sigh. "I wore them out," he announced. "Eight kids between them, and they couldn't handle it. They gave up the ghost." But he had a big grin on his face.

"So have you started on number three now?" she asked. "Surely you're good for another four kids."

He guffawed loudly and slapped his thigh. "Aren't you a fun one," he said. "No, my heart died with the last one and just can't go through that kind of loss anymore."

"I'm sorry," she said with a smile. "I do hear you about the losses." She motioned at Marsha's house beside him and said, "I understand she lost her husband too."

"Yep, sure did," he said. "And what a fight that was."

She looked at him and raised her eyebrows. "You heard them fighting?"

"Yep," he said. "That's a funny one. He had an affair with another man. It was the darndest thing. You should have heard Marsha rip into him."

At that, Doreen's jaw dropped. "Seriously?"

He laughed. "Not what you'd think, would you? That guy was huge, six foot tall. And all I could hear was her screaming at him for having sex with a man." He chuckled and shook his head. "The world ain't what it used to be."

"I wonder who it was," she said.

"Not sure," he said. "They stormed around. Last I heard, he packed up some bags and got in his vehicle, then drove off. She never had him back again."

"No," Doreen said with a nod. "Not sure I'd want my husband back after that either."

"You got to marry the right kind of guy," he said. He looked over at her and grinned. "Are you still available?"

"Well, I'm back available again, if you want to put it that way," she said with a beaming smile. "But I'll be choosing my second partner a whole lot more carefully than I did the first."

"Sometimes life is like that," he said. "I chose well both times. But I lost the first one in childbirth and that was really, really tough. What I didn't realize was how hard it was raising four kids alone. I married very quickly after that, but I'm lucky because she was a lovely lady too." He headed back toward his property, and, at his gate, he turned and smiled and said, "Thank you again."

"Not a problem," she said. "I was looking into poor Marsha's kiwi contest stuff when I decided to come down for a walk."

"Oh, she's got some kiwis growing in her backyard," he said. "Of course she cheats."

Doreen froze, looked at him, and said, "In what way?"

"Well, she has this portable greenhouse that she covers the plants with as soon as it gets anywhere close to being cool and leaves them in the ground. She also said she has some special nutrients, but I don't know what that means. So, even though she says she doesn't greenhouse them over the summer, she does."

"Right," Doreen said with a nod. "That makes a simple kind of sense."

"Very simple when you think about it," he said. "I thought there for a while that she was moving the greenhouse, but then I realized she had this contraption that she made herself that kept the temperatures really nice and warm in there. Her kiwis have been doing lovely ever since."

"And yet they're hardy to a certain extent, but more warmth in spring can be a huge help," she said, hands on her hips, frowning. Mugs was wandering back and forth at the old guy's feet. He bent down and gave Mugs a good scratch, and then laughed when he saw the cat too.

"Not too many people walk with their cats," he muttered.

"All my animals love to come with me," she said. And Thaddeus, who'd been at her neck, tucked up for the most part under her hair, rose up to his full height. He fluttered his feathers and said, "Thaddeus is here. Thaddeus is here."

The old guy looked at him in astonishment. "You know something? My eyes aren't so great," he said. "I didn't even know he was there."

"Thaddeus is a bit of a character in his own right," she said with a chuckle.

"Well, you be careful," he said. "I'd avoid her if I were you. Anybody who cheats at something like a county fair contest …"

"Right. I hear you," she said.

He smiled and said, "If you're ever looking to be wife number three …" And, with a cackle, he headed back in and closed the gate firmly in her face. Still smiling, she walked past Marsha's place, understanding completely what he meant about a portable greenhouse. So, she was cheating, and that's why Rosie was so upset. But was it something to kill over? Not likely. Doreen wandered back to her house, and, as soon as she got in, she could feel the hunger pangs start again. Which didn't make any sense. She'd had a huge omelet and cream puffs. However, as she went inside, she decided that coffee was probably better.

Mack called just about then. "Hey," she said. "By the way, Marsha did cheat."

"What?" he asked, as if distracted, as if this kiwi thing

was the last thing on his mind.

She quickly explained what she'd learned about kiwis and Marsha's gardening technique. "And, by the way, Marsha's husband," she said, "apparently had an affair with another guy."

There was silence on the other end, and then Mack said, "Wow. You do get around, don't you?"

"I think that's the term for the husband," she said drily. "Me, I'm out visiting with people."

Chapter 27

Wednesday Late Afternoon ...

"DO YOU THINK it's related?" Doreen couldn't help asking Mack.

"It's hard to say," he said. "We do have some toxicology back, and they were all given a chemical drug. It does induce heart attacks without anybody knowing."

"Instantaneous?"

"Within a few minutes," he said. "Fifteen minutes, maybe ten, depending on what activity level."

"So why?" she asked. "How were they administered?"

"Likely from a drink," he said.

"Would they have knowingly done something like that?"

"It's pretty tasteless, so it could have easily been in their coffee or tea or juice."

"So anybody who is a common drinker or was meeting somebody could have had it and then potentially rushed away, so nobody would know."

"It's possible," he said. "It does take a little bit to get to the point of killing you."

"So we need to know who saw them the last time they had something to eat or drink."

"Believe it or not," he said, "we do know how to do our jobs."

"Right," she said. "I'd like to know who it was who first met them though."

"Well, so far, we're not getting too much in the way of answers."

"Maybe not," she said, "but I do think it's all surrounding Marsha."

"I wouldn't be so sure about that," he said. "She doesn't have any motive for killing the others."

"Kiwis?" she asked slowly.

"I highly doubt it's enough."

"Right," she said, groaning. "Maybe it's more about Rosie."

"Maybe, but then what does she have to do with anything? Just because Marsha's husband had an affair with another man, why should Marsha hate Rosie?"

"Unless it's Rosie's husband who Marsha's husband had the affair with?"

There was another silence on the other end as Mack contemplated that. "And that won't be something easy to prove."

"No," she said. Then she remembered the little book she put in the freezer. She walked over to the freezer, pulled it out, and opened it. "Aha, it worked," she said triumphantly.

"What worked?"

"Those pages from that address book that were stuck together?" she said. "Nan told me to put it in the freezer because, if it was gum, it would separate." And she flicked off the gum into the trash. "And the pages definitely are open now."

"And does it say anything?"

"It has Marsha's name. Interesting."

"Anything else?"

"Some numbers," she said, "but I'm not sure what they mean. Hang on. I'll take a photo, and then I'll call you right back." She hung up from Mack, took a photo, and sent it to him. And then she called him back. "Not sure what those mean though."

"No, I'm not sure either," he said. "I think I'll take a look into her bank account." With that, he hung up.

Doreen wondered if it wasn't blackmail. She stared at the numbers and wondered if Rosie was the sweet innocent person who she had appeared to be. Doreen hated to think badly of anyone, but what if, just what if she'd had something to do with blackmailing Marsha about her husband's infidelity? Marsha didn't look like the person who would want to have anybody know about her husband's proclivities. But that was a long time ago, so why would anybody care? But it was hard to say.

Doreen sat here, wondering about it, until, all of a sudden, she looked at that number and figured it out. She kept pacing the house now because her mind was caught on an angle that she hadn't really expected. Would Mack tell her if blackmail deposits were in Rosie's account? Or could it have been the other way around? Maybe Rosie had been forced to pay Marsha. Somewhat like Heidi had to pay Aretha in the end. And then Doreen thought further about it and shook her head and said, "No, there's got to be something more to this."

Marsha would tell her though. Doreen was sure of that. But why would Marsha care about something like that one decade later? Obviously there were a lot of reasons to care, but how would it possibly have anything to do with the other dead women? After all, the four dead women were killed with the same chemical drug. Doreen was so close to tying this together. Yet she was missing something …

Just then Nan called. "So I heard about a conversation," she said. "I don't know if it has anything to do with anything, but the grandson apparently was yelling at Rosie about her husband's problems."

"His grandfather?"

"Yes. Apparently Danny is gay, so he believes that his grandfather might have been too. Rosie was denying it completely. She was in tears about the whole thing. But Danny said something about hearing from her friends that his grandfather was gay."

"Oh," Doreen said with a *thump* as she sat down. "What are the chances your Rosie wasn't anywhere near the same sweet old lady everybody thought she was?"

"I wouldn't believe it," Nan said stoutly. "She was always the sweetest."

"Maybe," Doreen said, "but maybe not." She sat here wondering how she was supposed to figure this out without hurting Nan's feelings or without spoiling her memories of her friend Rosie. "Nan, did Rosie ever have any heart medicine?"

"Of course she did," she said. "She did not have a bad heart, but it was a little bit of a slow ticker. She was supposed to take the medicine but wouldn't. Never did take it."

"What about her husband?"

"Now he had a heart condition," she said. "But I still don't know what happened to him."

"No," Doreen said, "but I have a really sad feeling I do."

"Are you going to tell me?"

"Not yet," she said. "I'll get back to you."

She tried to call Mack right back, but there was no answer. She sat here, considering her phone for a long moment. And then she decided she would call Marsha. She picked up the phone and dialed the woman. When she answered, she said, "This is Doreen, and I was just speaking with you in your garden."

"How did you get my number?" Marsha asked.

"Well, it's not that hard. You've been mentioned in all kinds of places, and there is still such a thing as a phone book," Doreen said in exasperation.

Marsha sniffed. "What do you want?" she asked.

"You didn't have anything to do with those four women's deaths, did you?"

"Of course not," she said. "Why would I?"

Her tone was authentically surprised. Doreen nodded. "Because there was some suggestion that maybe you might have killed them off in order to keep your kiwi-growing competition to yourself."

There was shocked silence first, and then Marsha started to laugh. "Oh my," she said. "I'm really not that much of a killer over my kiwis. My, my, my."

"Well, it was a thought that came up as everybody's connected to this contest."

"They were my friends," she said fiercely. "I never would have done anything to hurt them. You know how hard it is to have friends in this town?"

"Actually, I do," Doreen said. "I haven't had any luck meeting any myself."

"Well, if you weren't such a busybody," Marsha said, "you might have a chance of keeping friends."

"Ouch," Doreen said. "And, of course, you would have been pretty upset about the four women dying."

"Of course I was," she said. "It's been a tough-enough place to live after my husband's lovely little affair because, even though you want it to be kept quiet, it's pretty hard to do."

"Those women, of course, knew about the affair, didn't they?"

"They were the only ones I could talk to it about," Marsha admitted softly. "Rosie, on the other hand, was a whole different case."

"Right. She wanted to keep it secret, didn't she?"

"Yes. She didn't want anybody to know about it then, and neither did I," Marsha said. "Why would I? It was embarrassing and humiliating."

"And I'm sorry," she said, "because now I do understand a little bit more about how those four women died."

"Maybe," Marsha said suspiciously. "What is it to you anyway?"

"My grandmother was terribly worried over Rosie's death," Doreen said quietly. "I told her that I'd look into it. I also know that Rosie was asking me to look into a couple things too. She was upset about the other women's deaths as well."

"Well, I don't think she was upset about the women as much as she was upset about her husband," she snorted. "Personally, I think she killed them."

"Why would you think that?" Doreen asked. But privately she had wondered.

"Because they all knew about the affair, and they told her horrid grandson about it."

"Did they tell you that?"

"Yes, absolutely they did. Once Danny got ahold of that information, he would use it to blackmail his grandmother to get money out of her."

"That would have been tough," Doreen said sadly. "It's hard to imagine all the crimes committed over something that happened so long ago."

"It doesn't matter how long ago it happened," Marsha said, "because, the fact of the matter is, some of these things just never die. People won't let them die."

"Is that why you and Rosie didn't get along?"

"If you must know, my husband had an affair with Rosie's husband," she said, and the tears started to choke her throat.

"I'm so sorry," Doreen said. "That would have been particularly harsh. It's one thing to hear about it, but it's another thing to know who the person was."

"Exactly," she said. "Rosie didn't believe me for the longest time. I tried to tell her, and I tried to explain to her what had happened. But she wouldn't listen."

"And I understand that her husband just up and walked away too."

"No," Marsha said in a harsh voice. "Rosie killed him." With that, she hung up the phone.

Doreen stared at her phone in shock. She quickly dialed Mack, wishing and hoping that he would at least answer this time. When he finally came on the line, she said, "I just talked to Marsha. She said Rosie killed her husband too."

"What do you mean *too*?" Mack asked in exasperation. "Back up here a bit. Tell me exactly what happened."

"I will." Doreen quickly explained the conversation. "The thing is, by now, I don't know if she'll retract what she said because it was on the phone, and I had no way to record it."

"Of course not," Mack said. "Except for your little recorder at home."

Doreen snatched it up and saw it was on. She said, "Hang on a second." She hit Play, and the voices came back through again.

Mack sighed. "So, you do have a copy of it."

"Yeah," she said in shock, Goliath sitting here, staring at her. "I think Goliath may have walked on it. He may have just pressed the Play button while I was on the phone."

"Was the phone on Speaker?"

"Yes," she said. "It's giving me some trouble, so it was on Speakerphone."

"Well, it doesn't prove anything though," Mack said, "but we were wondering about Rosie because apparently Rosie's the last one to have seen two of the three other ladies."

"Who is the other one, not seen, that you know of?"

"Kimmy."

"Okay. Yes," Doreen said. "And I think that's because they told her gay grandson about his gay grandfather."

"And then who killed Rosie?"

"Well, we're not short of options," Doreen said with a heavy sigh. "Between Marsha's husband, if he's still alive, Marsha, and Rosie's grandson."

"And, of course, she could have committed suicide."

"But then why she be on her way to meet—"

"But everything is pinpointing and blaming Marsha, isn't it? Maybe Rosie decided that it was time to call it all quits before she got caught herself."

"Maybe," she said, "but Rosie was the fourth of the deaths. What about Kimmy's death? Nan said Kimmy did have a heart condition. So her having that chemical in her blood would be normal, right?"

"I've been checking on that too. At the moment, I'm not even sure Kimmy's death is connected," he said steadily. "It's possible hers was a natural death, and Rosie chose to kill off everybody else to make it look like they were all connected and to implicate Marsha."

"That would be a devious mind," she said. "Any idea what happened to her husband?"

"No. And we need to check out his community garden."

"Is he still alive?"

"Look. Let me make some calls," Mack said. "I'll talk to you later." He hung up.

At that, she quickly dialed the grandson and identified herself. "What do you want?" he said rudely.

"What I want," she said, "is to know where your grandmother's kiwi garden was."

"Why do you care?" he asked.

"Because I understand it had something to do with her son, your father."

"My father is dead," he said.

"How long ago was the accident?"

"A long time ago," he said. "And it was my father's plot of land that my grandmother used for her kiwis. It was a community garden, but she had a section off to the far side."

"So, is that where her kiwis are now?"

"I imagine so," he said. "I honestly don't know the difference."

"Well, she was pretty secretive about it."

"Of course she was. I don't even know if the kiwis are growing there."

"Maybe I could take a look," she said.

"Sure, fly at it," he said in a bored tone. And he gave her the address where it was.

"Thanks," she said.

It was already too late to go out tonight, but the next morning she planned to go first thing, bright and early.

Chapter 28

Thursday Early Morning...

WHEN DOREEN GOT up the next morning, she made coffee, put it in a thermos, called her animals to her, and headed out to the address. It wasn't too far to walk, but it was a good mile. By the time she got to the community garden, she was the only one there. Some of the individual plots of gardens were a riotous color of beautiful flowers. Others were vegetable gardens. She kept on walking through the gate to the back corner, where Danny had said his grandma's garden was located.

And, sure enough, a trellis was back there, and a long planter box with some vegetables and flowers were at the base. But definitely kiwi plants grew up along the trellis, where they would get direct sunlight. She didn't know about enough water because the fruits would need a tremendous amount of water to keep going. Mugs was interested in the box though. He kept straining at the leash to get closer.

Goliath, being Goliath, didn't seem to care. Thaddeus just watched Mugs as if unconcerned. Then why should he be? There were always a lot of people around here. As she stared down at the planter box, her phone rang. "Mack, what's up?"

"Where are you?" he asked.

"I'm looking at Rosie's kiwis," she said with a heavy sigh. "I think you need to come."

"Why?" he asked.

"Because I'm pretty sure I know why her kiwis are doing so wonderfully."

He groaned. "What does this have to do with anything?"

"Please come," she said, "and bring a shovel." And she hung up on him.

As she walked around the small garden, she wondered how simple and how ugly it could be. She hoped she was wrong. Not long afterward, when Mack's truck pulled up outside, she noted he wasn't in a RCMP car. She checked her watch and realized he hadn't even started his workday yet. He hopped out with a shovel in his hand and walked toward her, but his expression wasn't happy.

"I'm sorry," she said. Mugs wasn't. He barked and woofed, wagging his tail in joy at the sight of Mack. Even Goliath appeared to be excited as he ran to him.

"Mack is here," Thaddeus crowed in her ear. "Mack is here."

"I can see that," she muttered. "Too bad he isn't happy about it."

He glared at her as he straightened from greeting the animals. When he came nearer, he looked at the garden bed and shrugged and said, "So, what now?"

She pointed to the beautiful display of the small white kiwi flowers all along the back, growing along this big trellis.

"And?"

"I don't know how far down you have to dig," she said. "I doubt it'll be too far but just far enough ..."

"What will I find?"

She took a deep breath. "Rosie's husband."

He stared at her in shock.

She nodded quietly. "And I think I know what happened."

"You damn well better be wrong," he muttered. He looked at the raised bed, full of flowers and other plants. "Wouldn't we be disturbing all this?"

She nodded. "You could probably dig from this end," she muttered.

He quickly started digging down to the normal ground level and then below that. Over four and a half feet down, he stopped, wiped his brow, and said, "You better be right. I didn't need this today."

"None of us did," she snapped. She could feel the tension coiling deeper and deeper inside her as Mack dug farther.

Finally he stopped, shoveled out one round of dirt, and said, "You know what? We could dig this entire thing up and not find anything."

"But we won't have to," she said, as she leaned over and brushed off a bit of dirt.

And, sure enough, there was a white rounded bone. Looked like a toe.

He looked at it and swore a blue streak. He pulled out his phone, glared at her, and said, "Don't you move," as he called in a team.

Waiting for the team, Doreen was well past cold and tired. The animals were edgy and fussy, and she kept glaring at Mack, but he was ignoring her. Finally he walked over to her, and his glare had dimmed somewhat.

"I didn't mean to, you know," she snapped.

"Of course not," he said with a heavy sigh. "You never do."

"Now what?"

"Well, we'll exhume the body obviously. And you really think it's her husband?"

She nodded. "And I think she was blackmailing Marsha."

"Yes," he said. "I found the deposits in her bank account yesterday. We're still trying to track where it was coming from."

"That'll be easy," she said. "Check Marsha's account."

"So, why was Rosie getting money from Marsha?"

Doreen took a deep breath. "Well, if you want to go to Marsha's house, I'll show you."

He glared at her, then looked at the body and said, "Oh, hell no."

Doreen shrugged and said, "Okay. I won't tell you then."

He swore several more times.

She glared at him. "Do you realize what you're teaching Thaddeus?"

And out of Thaddeus's mouth came a blue streak that shocked her. Mack's jaw dropped. He looked at the bird, then looked at her, and a flush of red washed over his face. "I'm so sorry," he whispered. And Thaddeus repeated the blue streak of cursing again.

She reached up and tapped Thaddeus lightly at the beak. "No," she said.

He gave her a gimlet eye and said, "Thaddeus loves Nan."

"Oh, great. So you love Nan but not me?" she protested. He went and did his weird little cackling *ha-ha-ha* sound and tucked up against her neck. She walked toward Mack's truck and said, "Are you coming?"

"No, I'm not coming," he said. "I've had enough today."

"Okay," she said. "We'll talk later then."

She went to let herself out of the garden when he came racing behind her.

"Of course I'm coming," he roared. "Get into the damn truck."

"Get into the damn truck," Thaddeus immediately snapped.

Mack looked at Thaddeus, glared, and said, "Dammit."

"Dammit. Dammit," Thaddeus repeated.

"Stop," Doreen snapped at the top of her voice.

Both of them stared at her. She walked to the truck, shaking her head. "Don't bother apologizing anymore."

He got into the truck silently, while she helped Mugs up and then Goliath jumped up, not to be left alone. She hopped up with Thaddeus on her shoulder. In a quiet stew, Doreen was afraid that all she would hear from Thaddeus now would be swear words. And she knew who to blame for that.

Mack turned on the truck, reversed, and said, "Where am I going?"

She quickly gave him Marsha's address, then remained quiet for the rest of the drive. "You might as well go into the back here." She pointed at the alleyway. As they drove back there, he stopped at Marsha's gate. Doreen opened the truck door and walked into the backyard. Marsha was there, tending to her kiwis, removing her fancy little greenhouse apparatus. Caught in the act, she stopped, stared, and red washed over her face. "What are you doing here?" she cried out. "You can't trespass like that."

"No, maybe not," Doreen said. "That's a neat contraption, by the way, and a great way to make sure your kiwis grow really well."

The woman looked guiltily at the apparatus and then back at her kiwis. She moved it over and said, "Nobody said I'm not allowed to."

"Except for the fact that greenhouses aren't allowed," she said gently.

"It's hardly a greenhouse," she said, with an airy wave over to the greenhouse beside her. "That's a greenhouse." As if any idiot should know the difference.

Doreen nodded. "I get it," she said. She walked over to the kiwis, smiled, and nodded. "It's amazing. Rosie's looked quite similar though."

"You've seen her kiwis?" she asked eagerly. "How do they look?"

"I have. And they looked great," she said. "She copied you in more ways than you realize."

"What do you mean?" Marsha asked, but a note of fear was in her voice.

Doreen looked at Mack and said, "I'd suggest you start digging right here." She turned to look at Marsha and said, "And, of course, you don't object to us doing this, do you?"

"Of course I do," she said. "I don't want you digging anywhere near my roots. It'll totally destroy the kiwis."

"It will," she said. "But the fact of the matter is, there's something here we need to see."

Marsha immediately started to protest.

"Unless, of course, you want me to bring in the rest of the police team and the media," Doreen said in a firm tone.

Immediately Marsha closed her trap.

"And I can get a warrant," Mack said.

"How did you know?" Marsha asked in a faint whisper.

"Because we just found Rosie's husband under her kiwis."

All the color from Marsha's face drained completely away. She sat down with a hard *thump* on the corner of the raised bed. "Really?"

At Doreen's nod, Marsha whispered, "I didn't mean to. ... I was so upset when I found out what he'd done."

"He told you about his male lover, right?"

"Yes, while he was packing. Curtis said they would run away together."

"And then David was having a similar conversation with Rosie at the same time, I presume?"

"I don't know what happened to him. But Curtis? I lost my temper. ... And it was just rage. I was just so upset. I was out here, in the garden, and that red fury was building up so strong that, when he had finished packing, he came outside to say goodbye. And I reached up with my shovel and smacked him hard on the side of his head. He dropped like a log, and I basically folded him into the garden," she said, staring at the kiwis. "And a really weird thing happened over the years. The kiwis did better and better and better."

Doreen could just imagine. Talk about natural fertilizer. "And did Rosie kill her husband right away too?"

"I have no idea. I don't know about Rosie. But I don't think so."

"And how did Rosie know that Curtis was buried in your kiwis?"

"I said something once. That I had a particularly rich source of nutrients for the plants," she said sadly. "I didn't mean to, but I needed to tell somebody. And I think she understood. She said she was trying to settle up the divorce with her husband. Now I know that to be a lie. We were not really friends, but we were cordial enemies back then. After all, we had bonded over our shared experience."

"One that led to blackmail, I presume?"

Marsha nodded slowly.

"Well, I'm sure we'll find out that Rosie's husband died of a heart attack brought on by his own heart medicine that he had left at her place," Doreen said. "And it was all good, and both of you were content to keep your husbands out of the way and out of your lives. Until Rosie's grandson found out."

At that, Marsha winced. "Did Rosie really kill them? All three of them?"

"I think so, yes, because they knew about your husbands' gay affair, even if the other women didn't know about your husbands' deaths," she said. "Plus, I think Rosie committed suicide herself."

"Why would she do that?" Marsha cried out quietly.

Mack suggested an answer. "That's easy," he said. "She had just received a pretty rough diagnosis that her cancer was back."

"Oh my," Marsha said sadly. "Yes, she would have done that to avoid going through the chemo and radiation again."

"And she left a trail leading to you," Doreen said quietly.

Marsha stared up at her. "I really didn't mean to kill Curtis," she said.

"Maybe not," Doreen said. "But, the end result is, we've got six dead bodies all because of one extramarital affair."

"Not just an affair," Marsha said in a very sad tone. "A homosexual affair. You know what it's like to realize that your husband who you've shared your bed with for all those years prefers men? It's something that you can't even begin to fathom unless it happens to you. It's just so horrifying. ... It's more than a betrayal. Any affair is a betrayal, but this? This was like nothing else."

Marsha sniffled. "I'm sorry he's dead and gone," she said, "but I'm not sorry that I managed to bury that secret for all these years. It's the only way I could put one foot in front of the other in this town. So, as much as you may judge me for it, I don't feel like I have anything else to say."

"Except for one thing," Doreen said. "I don't understand why you put the flowers at Rosie's memorial site."

"Because, in many ways," Marsha said, "she was the only one who understood. Nobody else could even come close to understanding what I've gone through except her because she had been through the exact same thing."

"Right," Doreen said. She turned to look at Mack. "Satisfied?"

"Hardly," he said, his gaze on the older woman, who sat crushed against the flower bed. "I have an awful lot of questions still. Like Rosie's will for one." Mack turned to Doreen. "And why would Rosie come to you?"

"Her grandson really had terrorized her, and, after all the fighting," Doreen said, "I'm sure she was happy to give her estate to anybody but him. Plus she wanted me to know what she'd done. What Marsha had done."

"Any money she had left should be my money," Marsha said bitterly. "All these years, I paid her to keep quiet about me killing Curtis, and yet I shouldn't have. She'd killed her own husband too." At that, she started to laugh out loud in a horrifically loud cackle. And then, just as quickly, it went from laughter to tears.

Doreen walked over and gave the woman a hug.

Mack stared at the two of them. "This is just too unbelievable."

Still holding the now-weeping Marsha, Doreen looked at him. "Are you so sure I should focus on gardening as a hobby? Apparently growing kiwis is a killer."

Epilogue

Saturday Late Morning ...

TWO DAYS LATER Doreen walked away from the graveside. Rosie had been buried, after her autopsy stated her death a suicide, having ingested the remainder of her husband's old heart medicine and a cocktail of other drugs she'd had.

That wasn't why she would be remembered though. No, she had been accused of killing the other three women, and her husband, David, which had the entire community up in arms—not to mention the added news of Marsha going to jail for murdering her husband too.

Doreen had quietly stepped out of the hype reverberating around town. She watched as Nan walked away ahead of her. She would go to a celebration-of-life ceremony, which Doreen had also backed away from, hoping to go home and to just relax.

The last few days had been more media sensation than anything. The police were still trying to piece together the bits and pieces from Rosie's life, but it was a pretty simple case where the same drugs had been used in all three of the women's deaths, the first one having been an accident, and

257

Rosie using that as an opportunity to point fingers at Marsha and to take out women she considered her enemies.

The return of her cancer had apparently given her the freedom to make a few changes in her life—such as getting rid of the kiwi clique that had been a pain in her butt. And gave her a supposedly perfect opportunity to point the finger at the one other woman who could ruin her life by telling everyone what their husbands had done. Rosie had never wanted her grandson to know and had lived in fear of what he'd do if he found out. And the police had found the same drug had been given to her husband, whom she'd killed years ago. It looked like it was a pretty simple open-and-shut case, but the end result had left the community in shock.

And, of course, the county fair would never be the same again.

As Doreen walked by the multiple fresh graves, she stopped to look at various stones and monuments, seeing patches of lilies at various places.

Finally she ended up in a complete circle, as she stood over Rosie's grave. "I hope you're at peace now," she said sadly. "It's not the end I would have wanted for you."

And she reached out and picked up a lily, sniffed it, wondering why lilies always represented death. As far as she was concerned, flowers should be for life and rebirth. But so often they were used for funerals. She placed it back into the vase and straightened.

She didn't have the animals with her, out of respect for the others attending the ceremonies dotting the cemetery. It's a good thing she'd left them at home, as signs were everywhere, saying No Pets Allowed. But being without them? ... Well, she felt a little lost herself.

Not to mention how worried she was about this afternoon's meeting with Mack's lawyer brother. But she'd dragged out as much time as she could here. She needed to go home and eat before the two men arrived, and she had to face the unpleasantness of her now-defunct marriage.

She stared at the lilies for one last long moment, sighed, and turned to step away. As she did, a shadow fell over her side, and she could feel somebody reaching out for her. She turned with a smile, only to cry out at the blow that came out of nowhere and struck her on the back of her head. She didn't hear anything but the sounds of footsteps thundering away, as she crashed into the pile of lilies at the graveside.

The pain was crushing. The shock paralyzing.

Poor Mack. He would be the one to find her.

Lilies. How appropriate.

Her last thought before the blackness took her over? She had already come up with a name for the investigation into her own death.

Lifeless in the Lilies.

This concludes Book 11 of Lovely Lethal Gardens: Killer in the Kiwis.

Read about Lifeless in the Lilies: Lovely Lethal Gardens, Book 12

Lovely Lethal Gardens: Lifeless in the Lilies (Book #12)

A new cozy mystery series from *USA Today* best-selling author Dale Mayer. Follow gardener and amateur sleuth Doreen Montgomery—and her amusing and mostly lovable cat, dog, and parrot—as they catch murderers and solve crimes in lovely Kelowna, British Columbia.

Riches to rags. … Chaos calms. … Suddenly it's quiet. … Too quiet if Doreen's involved!

What was supposed to be a leisurely stroll through a peaceful cemetery after a recent funeral turns into the start of a new case. Someone clobbers Doreen over the head and leaves her facedown among the funeral flowers.

Is it random violence? Revenge? A warning of worse to come?

No one knows, not even Doreen, but one thing is certain: the attack enabled the disappearance—perhaps the abduction?—of Doreen's beloved African gray parrot, Thaddeus. Frantic, Doreen foregoes a trip to the emergency room in favor of heading straight home, where she hopes Thaddeus will return sooner rather than later.

But when he does, the bird sports an SOS message fastened around his ankle, leading Doreen to a odd corner of town and a curious little boy who know one will talk about.

Now someone is leaving threats on Doreen's doorstep and then delivering threats in person …

Between birds and boys and Corporal Mack Moreau's brother, the lawyer looking into her divorce situation, Doreen has her hands full. And that's before her former lawyer shows up unexpectedly at her home! Off-balance by all these events, Doreen opens her door to someone with a serious grudge to take her down …

Find Book 12 here!

To find out more visit Dale Mayer's website.

https://smarturl.it/DMSLillies

Get Your Free Book Now!

Have you met Charmin Marvin?

If you're ready for a new world to explore, and love ill-mannered cats, I have a series that might be your next binge read. It's called Broken Protocols, and it's a series that takes you through time-travel, mysteries, romance... and a talking cat named Charmin Marvin.

Go here and tell me where to send it!
http://smarturl.it/ArsenicBofB

Author's Note

Thank you for reading Killer in the Kiwis: Lovely Lethal Gardens, Book 11! If you enjoyed the book, please take a moment and leave a short review.

Dear reader,

I love to hear from readers, and you can contact me at my website: www.dalemayer.com or at my Facebook author page. To be informed of new releases and special offers, sign up for my newsletter or follow me on BookBub. And if you are interested in joining Dale Mayer's Reader Group, here is the Facebook sign up page.
https://smarturl.it/DaleMayerFBGroup

Cheers,
Dale Mayer

About the Author

Dale Mayer is a USA Today bestselling author best known for her Psychic Visions and Family Blood Ties series. Her contemporary romances are raw and full of passion and emotion (Second Chances, SKIN), her thrillers will keep you guessing (By Death series), and her romantic comedies will keep you giggling (It's a Dog's Life and Charmin Marvin Romantic Comedy series).

She honors the stories that come to her – and some of them are crazy and break all the rules and cross multiple genres!

To go with her fiction, she also writes nonfiction in many different fields with books available on resume writing, companion gardening and the US mortgage system. She has recently published her Career Essentials Series. All her books are available in print and ebook format.

Connect with Dale Mayer Online

Dale's Website – www.dalemayer.com
Facebook Personal – https://smarturl.it/DaleMayerFacebook
Instagram – https://smarturl.it/DaleMayerInstagram
BookBub – https://smarturl.it/DaleMayerBookbub
Facebook Fan Page – https://smarturl.it/DaleMayerFBFanPage
Goodreads – https://smarturl.it/DaleMayerGoodreads

Also by Dale Mayer

Published Adult Books:

Hathaway House

Aaron, Book 1

Brock, Book 2

Cole, Book 3

Denton, Book 4

Elliot, Book 5

Finn, Book 6

Gregory, Book 7

Heath, Book 8

Iain, Book 9

Jaden, Book 10

Keith, Book 11

Lance, Book 12

Melissa, Book 13

Nash, Book 14

Owen, Book 15

Hathaway House, Books 1–3

Hathaway House, Books 4–6

Hathaway House, Books 7–9

The K9 Files

Ethan, Book 1

Pierce, Book 2

Zane, Book 3

Blaze, Book 4

Lucas, Book 5

Parker, Book 6

Carter, Book 7

Weston, Book 8

Greyson, Book 9

Rowan, Book 10

Caleb, Book 11

Kurt, Book 12

Lovely Lethal Gardens

Arsenic in the Azaleas, Book 1

Bones in the Begonias, Book 2

Corpse in the Carnations, Book 3

Daggers in the Dahlias, Book 4

Evidence in the Echinacea, Book 5

Footprints in the Ferns, Book 6

Gun in the Gardenias, Book 7

Handcuffs in the Heather, Book 8

Ice Pick in the Ivy, Book 9

Jewels in the Juniper, Book 10

Killer in the Kiwis, Book 11

Lifeless in the Lilies, Book 12

Lovely Lethal Gardens, Books 1–2

Lovely Lethal Gardens, Books 3–4

Lovely Lethal Gardens, Books 5–6

Lovely Lethal Gardens, Books 7–8

Lovely Lethal Gardens, Books 9–10

Psychic Vision Series

Tuesday's Child

Hide 'n Go Seek

Maddy's Floor
Garden of Sorrow
Knock Knock…
Rare Find
Eyes to the Soul
Now You See Her
Shattered
Into the Abyss
Seeds of Malice
Eye of the Falcon
Itsy-Bitsy Spider
Unmasked
Deep Beneath
From the Ashes
Stroke of Death
Ice Maiden
Psychic Visions Books 1–3
Psychic Visions Books 4–6
Psychic Visions Books 7–9

By Death Series
Touched by Death
Haunted by Death
Chilled by Death
By Death Books 1–3

Broken Protocols – Romantic Comedy Series
Cat's Meow
Cat's Pajamas
Cat's Cradle
Cat's Claus
Broken Protocols 1-4

Broken and... Mending

Skin

Scars

Scales (of Justice)

Broken but... Mending 1-3

Glory

Genesis

Tori

Celeste

Glory Trilogy

Biker Blues

Morgan: Biker Blues, Volume 1

Cash: Biker Blues, Volume 2

SEALs of Honor

Mason: SEALs of Honor, Book 1

Hawk: SEALs of Honor, Book 2

Dane: SEALs of Honor, Book 3

Swede: SEALs of Honor, Book 4

Shadow: SEALs of Honor, Book 5

Cooper: SEALs of Honor, Book 6

Markus: SEALs of Honor, Book 7

Evan: SEALs of Honor, Book 8

Mason's Wish: SEALs of Honor, Book 9

Chase: SEALs of Honor, Book 10

Brett: SEALs of Honor, Book 11

Devlin: SEALs of Honor, Book 12

Easton: SEALs of Honor, Book 13

Ryder: SEALs of Honor, Book 14

Macklin: SEALs of Honor, Book 15

Heroes for Hire

SEALs of Steel

The Mavericks

Kerrick, Book 1

Griffin, Book 2

Jax, Book 3

Beau, Book 4

Asher, Book 5

Ryker, Book 6

Miles, Book 7

Nico, Book 8

Keane, Book 9

Lennox, Book 10

Gavin, Book 11

Shane, Book 12

Bullard's Battle Series

Ryland's Reach, Book 1

Cain's Cross, Book 2

Eton's Escape, Book 3

Garret's Gambit, Book 4

Kano's Keep, Book 5

Fallon's Flaw, Book 6

Quinn's Quest, Book 7

Bullard's Beauty, Book 8

Collections

Dare to Be You…

Dare to Love…

Dare to be Strong…

RomanceX3

Standalone Novellas

It's a Dog's Life

Riana's Revenge
Second Chances

Published Young Adult Books:

Family Blood Ties Series
Vampire in Denial
Vampire in Distress
Vampire in Design
Vampire in Deceit
Vampire in Defiance
Vampire in Conflict
Vampire in Chaos
Vampire in Crisis
Vampire in Control
Vampire in Charge
Family Blood Ties Set 1–3
Family Blood Ties Set 1–5
Family Blood Ties Set 4–6
Family Blood Ties Set 7–9
Sian's Solution, A Family Blood Ties Series Prequel
    Novelette

Design series
Dangerous Designs
Deadly Designs
Darkest Designs
Design Series Trilogy

Standalone
In Cassie's Corner
Gem Stone (a Gemma Stone Mystery)

Published Non-Fiction Books:

Career Essentials

Career Essentials: The Résumé
Career Essentials: The Cover Letter
Career Essentials: The Interview
Career Essentials: 3 in 1